STEPHEN KING

GRAVE

DECISIONS

Grave Decisions

Don't let your last decision be the wrong one.
Follow the terror and drama in five short stories that will
bring you gravely close to your fears.
The winds are howling, can you hear the screams?

Copyright © 2016 by Stephen King

Manufactured in the United States of America
Designed by Magic Pen Designs

Contents:

Grave Decisions

Pale Jesse rode the plains some hundred and fifty years ago. If, indeed, he ever rode at all. He was a legend – the only one that the little town of Kitchener had – and his name was something children all over the area knew. Kitchener was a tiny place in America's backyard, a place that was only ever visited on the way to somewhere else. For the people who lived there, it would always be their home. No one ever came, and no one ever left. There was one post office, one gym, one bank, one church and one school.

And in that school, every Kitchener child learned the name of Pale Jesse. They performed his story in plays every year, and each year some teacher or other took it upon themselves to adjust the legend to their own personal taste. The adjustments had gone on for so many generations that no one could be entirely sure what the original tale of Pale Jesse was anymore. All they knew was what he looked like, and what he carried with him on his adventures in the Wild West.

Jesse was a tall creature with features that belied neither boy nor man. A springy adolescent with a thin frame hanging on even thinner bones, Pale Jesse got his namesake from the lily-white hue of his skin. The color was usually associated with cowards in the West, but this rider carved out a rather bloodthirsty history for himself nonetheless. Jesse carried with him a long lasso rope, and it was reputed that he was an expert at hooking and strangling his enemies, even from several feet away. He also wore a long, curved knife on his belt, and when his victims were dead – or at least very nearly dead – Jesse would carve a widened smile onto their faces, splitting the corners of their lips.

"A happy little visit from Pale Jesse."

This was what all the old-timers joked when they wanted to frighten the children a little. All except one.

The padre was seventy-five, and he wasn't a fan of jokes about legendary murderers. Pale Jesse was a name that never crossed the lips of anyone within his glorious church, though he knew they'd all talked about the wild rider at some time or other. The padre felt it prudent, however, to make sure they knew that such names being mentioned in the presence of God was a sacrilegious offence. And God, as they all ought to have known, is everywhere.

This had been the way of things, until that sweltering Friday morning in August. It was the kind where the backs of your knees stuck together with sweat, and the padre had been clamouring for shade on his wide porch. A glass of ice cold lemonade was slowly turning tepid in his grip. On that damned Friday, Mrs. Fiona Haverford came running up his steps. In her scrawny arms, she held a new-fangled laptop computer, and her face was white as a sheet despite the burning glory of the Lord's sunshine.

"Padre!" she called, her voice shrill and a little broken. "Padre, it's my daughter Michaela!"

The old minister eyed the laptop, and at once his mind went to the many new sins available to teenagers thanks to the Internet. He had consulted the World Wide Web himself to find out how to protect Kitchener's young from the evils of the online world, only to end up with a pornographic pop-up on his desktop that wouldn't go away. Mrs. Fiona Haverford stood waiting, and the padre let a small grumble out as he got up from his chair. The lemonade was left to boil over in the sun. It would stay there for days before the padre remembered to clean it away.

Once inside the padre's lavish home, Fiona took the laptop to the table. She faced it away from the sun, into the dark recesses of the dining room, and pushed a button to wake the machine from its slumber. The padre fumbled in his pockets for his glasses, settling the thin, silver-rimmed frames over his aged, bulbous nose. They sat together, dark-wood chairs side by side, and Fiona double-clicked on a file marked: VIDEO_AUTOSAVE001. The screen took the shape of a black box, framed by various controls, and a moment later, a video was playing.

It was Michaela Haverford, in all her thirteen year old glory. The girl held a guitar and she was adjusting the camera to frame herself properly within its reach. She sat cross-legged on the end of her bed, the blanket that her grandmother had made for her beneath her. The padre remembered Old Mrs. Haverford stitching the patchwork at church lunches, all those years ago when Fiona was expecting the girl. Time had flown, Michaela had sprouted like a beanpole, and now she was starting to sing and play her music.

"If you're concerned that her songs aren't Godly enough..." the padre began wearily.

But Fiona shook her head. Her hand had risen to cover her mouth, her eyes glued to the screen even when she replied to the old minister.

"She's got one of those YouTube channels going, padre, for her country music," Fiona said with stunted breaths, "and that's just fine. But...something happened to her last night. Something awful. And the camera caught it - she was in the middle of recording when it happened."

"When *what* happened, my child?" the padre asked.

Fiona would not answer. She only pointed to the screen, and the man of God sat and watched as the girl's voice grew in confidence and volume. Her young face was freckled and pretty, her eyes a dreamy young shade of blue. Michaela was happy and melodious, like most other kids when left to their own dreams and devices. Knowing that something terrible was about to happen tied the padre's guts in a knot. He waited, the words of the songs drifting right over his head.

Until Michaela suddenly stopped singing.

She ended mid-sentence, and the guitar slipped out of her grip as though she'd lost control of her hands. Michaela appeared to be looking at something behind the camera, as if someone had entered her room. She shuffled back on the bed, her grandmother's blanket creasing in a heap. Michaela shook her head, over and over again. All at once, the color had drained from her face, and those dream-filled eyes were pale with terror. The padre tried to follow the pattern of her gaze, for now her focus seemed to be closer. She was looking at something right in front of her, but the camera showed nothing at all for her to be afraid of.

"P-p-p-p..." Michaela stammered.

Fiona let a sob escape her lips. She was shaking, trying to hold all her horror in to watch her baby girl grow so afraid. The padre was afraid too, though he knew not why.

"P-p-p-p..." The girl said again. She was trying to speak, but her voice was paralyzed by fear.

In the dark dining room, Fiona raised a bony hand. Her finger shook as she pointed, and she finally looked away from the screen.

When her eyes met the padre's, they were exactly the same fearful shade as her daughter's.

"Listen," Fiona told him. She closed her eyes tightly, her head turned away.

On the screen, Michaela took a deep, shaky breath. She pointed too, straight at a space not a foot from where she was cowering on her bed.

"P-p-p...Pale Jesse!" she cried.

And then it happened. The padre watched as Michaela's body shook with a violent force. She gasped, a deep whooping gasp of air, and then clutched at her throat as if something had rammed its way down her windpipe. Choking and spluttering, Michaela fought with an invisible force, writhing on the bed and screaming for help. She thrashed and thrashed, breaking her lampshade and throwing the room into semi-darkness. The only light was the faint blue glow given off by her laptop, and it showed the girl's continued battle with her own body.

And then she was still.

For one awful moment, the padre was convinced she had died from her strange seizure. But to his surprise and relief, Michaela was slowly getting up. She clambered onto her hands and knees, and her heavy breaths became slower, more controlled. Michaela crawled back to the laptop, settling again on the corner of her now-disheveled bed. Her hair fell about her face, disguising it for a moment as she contemplated the floor. Then, she looked up, and the padre let a gasp of his own escape.

"Her eyes," he breathed.

Michaela's eyes were black, from pupil to iris and beyond. There was no other color in her gaze, and no way to mistake the fact that they were so. The padre had never seen anything like it before. He watched, dumbfounded, as Michaela snapped her laptop shut and killed the video recording instantly. In the padre's dining room, the laptop reverted to the black box of the video player, as if nothing bad had even happened. This was what the padre despised so much about technology, its cold, unfeeling nature.

"She's still like that, padre," Fiona whispered. Her face was covered by her hands, and her sobs were finally spilling out in bursts and shrieks. "We kept her off school today, and she's tucked up in bed. She hasn't spoken since that night, and her eyes are black as the pits of Hell. I don't know what to do. We need you, padre."

That was Friday morning, the Friday when everything changed. On Friday afternoon, the padre found himself at Burt's Hardware Store on the only shopping street that Kitchener town had. His aged, hunched form had straightened a little, boosted by the force of the mission he now had to fulfill. It was clear a demon had settled in the poor young vessel that was Michaela Haverford, and there was only one man of God who could set that right. She had named her demon as Pale Jesse, but that was just kids talking. They used Pale Jesse for the name of any ghost or spooky phenomena they couldn't explain. The truth was far more terrifying: a servant of Satan had come to town.

The padre could not find what he was looking for in Burt's, so he went to the counter to inquire. The Burt who now owned the store, like the three generations of Burt's before him, was a tall, stocky fellow with a barrel chest and arms like zeppelins.

"What can I do ya for, padre?" he asked cheerily.

There was no cheer in the minister's voice as he replied, "I need nails, Burt. Long, rusty nails. I've got me an exor…a, uh, project to take care of," he said and tried to stop himself from blurting out anything else.

****

On the other side of town, which was still within screaming distance of the padre and Burt's place, there was a small collection of disused farm buildings. The farm owner, one Elias Heck, had let the old place fall into disrepair a few years back, when his wife was taken ill.

They were an elderly couple who had spent their lives tending the farm and fostering children, on account of not being able to conceive any of their own. The children of Heck Farm were the only new faces to ever come and go from Kitchener, though many of them stayed in town once they were eighteen.

When Mrs. Heck died of her illness, she and Elias were taking care of a boy the townspeople called Little Jimmy. He was nine years old, give or take, and his hair was black and cut short against his little head. By all accounts small for his age, Little Jimmy made up for this shortcoming in the brains department. He was excellent at mathematics and smart as a whip at figuring out all things mechanical. Most of the time he spent at the farm was in the decomposing barns, tinkering with old tractors and the like.

Elias Heck wasted away after his wife passed. He had been dead inside the farmhouse for about four weeks, and Little Jimmy had decided it was best not to tell anyone just yet. It had been enough of a nasty shock for the town to hear of Mrs. Heck's passing, let alone that her husband had followed her just over a month later. Little Jimmy had thrown a blanket over the old man's corpse, where he had died in his rocking chair with a bottle of whiskey clutched to his chest. Jimmy tiptoed past it every time he went to the kitchen, as if old Elias was merely sleeping.

He was starting to smell, though, and that was going to be a problem. When the smell was only contained in the living room, Little Jimmy had been able to suck in his breath while passing through. When the contamination took the whole of downstairs, it was time to wear one of the protective face masks Elias used to wear when he sprayed chemicals on the fields. But once the smell was everywhere in the house, Little Jimmy had decided to move into one of the barns. He'd stopped getting food from the kitchen anyway and dug into the cellar stores so he didn't even have to go inside.

In the early morning light on Friday, a few hours before the school bus was due to pick him up, Little Jimmy took a sleeping bag and some blankets over to the barn. He had picked a fine spot out for himself, on a high shelf that was still filled with dry, warm hay. Jimmy loved the barn, with its smell of tractor oil and the sight of tools strewn everywhere, and he didn't mind settling on the hay in the least. Before he was fostered by the Hecks, he'd slept in an unlocked, beaten-up car out on the streets of Queens, while his mother got fucked for money inside their studio apartment. The barn was infinitely better, and Little Jimmy lay in the hay and smiled up at the ceiling for a contemplative moment.

"Well hello there, son," said a voice with a twang.

Little Jimmy didn't jump. He'd been through too much in his nine years to be surprised or afraid of strange voices. He merely rolled onto his side on the hay bed and looked down into the rest of the barn.

"Can I help you, Mister?" Jimmy asked.

Standing beside the tractor was a tall, thin man with very pale skin. He wore leather chaps over his trousers and big brown boots that must have walked thousands of miles. His white face was scarred and impossibly thin, and his hair shone red where it caught the sunlight. He could only have been ten years older than Little Jimmy at the most. On his hip he wore a long, curved knife that looked mighty sharp. And in his pale hands, he held a length of rope that resembled a lasso.

"Don't you know who I am, son?" the man replied.

Little Jimmy shook his head.

"I ain't been in Kitchener too long," the boy explained. "Only at school a couple months before the summer let out and only been back a few weeks again. I don't have no friends yet, and Mr. Heck don't like me to talk to adults without him. He says my New York manners ain't manners at all."

"I reckon he's probably right," the man answered. His pale face lifted into a thin smile. "Where is the old bastard?"

Jimmy bristled at the word. He'd liked Mr. Heck, and he didn't see any reason to call him names. "Elias is in the house," Jimmy said protectively. "He don't want to see nobody, on account of he's still grieving for Mrs. Martha Heck. She's passed."

"So Old Elias is the body under the blanket then," the man surmised.

Jimmy was horrified at the stranger's supposition. He stood up high on the shelf, trying to look intimidating as he bore down on the young man. Hands on his hips, Jimmy forced his voice to be loud and firm.

"How'd you get in our house?" he demanded. "That's criminal. I could call Officer Blake on you. Breaking and entering, that's the offence."

"I didn't break, I just entered," the man explained. "I go wherever I please, and there ain't nobody gonna stop me doin' that, kid."

Silence fell, and Jimmy's fear and rage made his small body tense.

"Quit yer worryin'," the man added with a small chuckle, "I ain't gonna tell nobody about your foster-pa being dead. They'd take you back to the agency then, wouldn't they Jimmy? You see, I know how this new-fangled foster business works. I watch and learn."

The young man tapped the side of his pale nose with an even paler finger. His shirt was made of coarse fabric, and as Jimmy observed him more closely, he realized the shirt was full of holes. All over his chest and stomach, little holes had been torn through the cloth by something no larger than a penny. When he noticed Jimmy's wandering eyes, the stranger slapped his thigh with a resounding echo.

"Where are those manners my momma tried to teach me?" the stranger asked. "I'm Jesse, since you don't know me. What's your name little man?"

"I was James in New York," the boy replied, "but here I'm Little Jimmy Heck."

"Why don't you come on down here, Little Jimmy Heck?" the stranger offered. "I got something I need to talk to you about."

It didn't sound like a good idea. Little Jimmy was mighty smart, and living in the dangerous backstreets of New York had made him wary of danger. He'd thought that Kitchener was a safe place, filled with sleepy people who never went anywhere or did anything much, but meeting Jesse had sparked something of the old red-alert in the little boy. He'd not felt this kind of trepidation since the night his mother was shot by gangsters. She'd been wearing a fine red dress, and the bullets had made holes in the fabric.

Holes.

Little Jimmy leaned over the precipice of the shelf again, looking at Jesse's shirt. The holes were the same as the ones in his mother's body, and that made a strange, familiar feeling settle amid his fears.

"Come on, James," Jesse offered, "we need to talk. I want to give you a purpose in this town. Wouldn't you like that? A job to do?"

"A job?" Jimmy asked. "Does it pay?"

"Whatever you find, you can keep," Jesse explained. "Plus, I won't go telling nobody that you've got a dead man in your living room."

That was pay enough, for if they discovered that Elias was dead, Jimmy knew he'd go back to the agency. He'd be sleeping on the stiff beds of the holding facility until they found him a new place to go. He liked Kitchener, it was small and everybody knew each other, nothing at all like New York. He didn't want to go back. He wanted to stay with the tractors and his schoolmates. They were putting on a play real soon, and his teacher, Miss Dupree, had already said that Jimmy would get the lead role. He didn't know who the character was yet, but he was excited all the same.

Jimmy climbed down the ladder from the shelf and stood facing Jesse. Up close, the young man was even thinner and paler than before. Jimmy had to wonder why he was still wearing a shirt with bullet holes in it when surely he could have bought something new. Jesse grinned, observing the boy from head to toe, then he held out a warning finger.

"First things first," he began. "When it gets dark tonight, you got to bury Old Elias. Folks are gonna smell him from the street soon otherwise. Go round the back of the farmhouse and get to diggin' a hole. Six foot long and as deep as you can manage. After that, we'll have work to do, you and me."

"Can't you help me?" Jimmy asked. "That sounds like a lot of labor for a little kid."

Jesse barked out a laugh and put his hands on his hips. "Aren't you a wily devil?" he countered. "I picked the right kid here, I'm sure of that. I wouldn't be a lot of help to you, kiddo. I ain't got the power I used to have."

And Little Jimmy might have agreed that Jesse was on the scrawny side, but the man had a knife and a lasso. He must have had some skills. Jimmy was about to protest again when Jesse raised a hushing finger to his lips. He shook his head slowly, and then he walked away. It was strange to see him heading straight for the wall opposite the tractor, like there was a door within the crumbling wood that only he could see. Jimmy watched with fascination as Jesse neared the wall, stopping only to look back over his shoulder and deliver a final message.

"Your momma says hello, by the way."

Then he walked straight *through* the barn wall, and he was gone.

****

"Thank you for coming, padre," Fiona Haverford stammered. "We kept our eyes on her all afternoon, just like you said."

"And there's been no change?" the padre asked.

The grieving mother shook her head.

"She's just lying there," she said. "No words, not even looking at us."

"But not asleep neither," said a second voice, equally fearful. "She's wide awake, eyes open and lookin' at the ceiling."

The second voice belonged to Mr. Buck Haverford, who had bitten all his nails down to the quick since the incident with Michaela. The padre was surprised to see Buck, a funeral director by trade, so struck down with fear and confusion. They often worked together to produce church funerals, most recently the ceremony for Mrs. Martha Heck, and Buck was a soul you could usually count on in a crisis. Now, he was a shell of himself, looking up the stairs as if the Devil himself had moved into the spare room. It was entirely possible he had, the padre reasoned. He put a hand on Buck's shoulder, patting gently.

"The Lord is with your family, Buck," he reassured him, "and with Michaela too."

"You think you can do it, padre?" Buck asked him, his voice laden with desperation. "You reckon you can out the demon from her?"

The padre's hand wandered to hover over his shoulder bag. Within the folds of leather, he had his bible. Nestled close to it were the long, rusty nails Burt had supplied, along with some lengths of rope, shards of wood, and a huge mallet that hadn't been used since the padre was still young enough to go camping. The man of God adjusted the bag on his shoulder, and his gaze was drawn up the stairs too.

"Satan is no match for our faith," the padre decreed, "you must pray and believe in that, always."

Fiona nodded and dropped to her knees where she was standing. Buck took a moment to catch on, but soon he too was murmuring holy words and down on all fours, bowing his head to an unseen master. The padre sidled between them, offering a silent blessing over their heads, then he climbed the stairs of their pleasant family home. All the way up the steps, he saw photographs of Michaela through the years. She was a sweet, bright thing, and every smiling picture made the padre's insides swirl with guilt. What he would have to do to bring the demon out would hurt Michaela.

But it had to be done.

Her bedroom was deathly quiet when the padre entered it, so quiet he had a moment where he felt certain she'd abandoned it. When the door swung open fully, he found her lying supine on her bed. Her parents had tucked her up in her grandmother's patchwork blanket, all the way up to where her little face peered out, perfectly still. Her freckles had faded. Her hair was astray at angles that a vain thirteen year old should have abhorred. And her eyes were dark as the night outside the window. No speck of illumination survived within their depths.

"Michaela, do you hear me child?" the padre asked.

No answer came, as he'd expected. The old preacher didn't like the silence, and he filled it with whispered prayers as he emptied the contents of his bag. He kept the bible away from Michaela and her wide, dark eyes, just in case the holy words sparked something before he was ready. The ropes were what he needed first, and he laid them out one by one over the patchwork blanket. The first part was easy. All he had to do was tie Michaela's hands and feet to the four short posts of the bed.

He disliked un-tucking the child from her cozy nest, least of all because it meant that his withered skin had to touch her ice-cold frame.

She was still wearing the clothes she'd had on for her music video, a cute cowgirl shirt and jeans. Somehow they didn't seem to fit anymore. The fabric hung loose and disheveled on Michaela's motionless frame. When the padre had secured her, he appraised his work, and then re-covered the girl with her blankets. Only her head, hands and feet stuck out of the bedclothes.

The padre still hoped the bible would be enough. He had consulted as many fellow preachers as he had phone numbers for, and all of them had told him the various passages and scripture selections that were sure to draw the demon forward. When confronted with the holy word of God, the beast would not be able to stay within the vessel of the innocent child. The rusty nails were a precaution, from an ancient holy man who had claimed to have performed a similar task in his youth. The padre said a prayer, asking the Lord not to make him have to use them.

"Demon, hear the word of the Father and be gone from this child!"

Citations and prayers passed his lips, each rising in timbre and volume. The padre tried every line he'd marked in his bible, yet the girl remained still. Her eyes were void as ever, and though she moved just a little, enough to tell that she was breathing, that motion was constant as the swell of a calm sea. The demon cared not for scripture, and that meant the only way forward was pain.

He didn't want to do it. He was a good man at heart, perhaps even a little of a coward. The padre placed the shards of wood – taken from a cross broken accidentally at Sunday service – under Michaela's hands and feet. He took one of the longest nails, observing the crusted orange corrosion that had grown like mould all over the metal. The nail was as cold as the child herself, rotten and unclean. The padre felt the weight of the hammer in his hand.

He lined the nail up with Michaela's palm, the wood ready to catch it underneath, and said one final prayer before he began his grim work.

Bang.

The first nail went through, and it was easier to do than he'd expected. Perhaps it was easy because Michaela still did not react despite the agonizing pain of impalement. Yet, as the padre lined up the second nail for the second palm, he thought he heard the voice of the Devil in his mind.

That's it, child of the Almighty, the voice crooned. *Do your good work. Bring that child pain, for it will only raise me to glory.*

Bang.

He hoped the sound would silence the demon, but laughter followed, echoing in the holy man's mind.

I shall be risen, padre. You shall bring it about.

Bang.

This child is my vessel; you shall not take her from me.

Bang.

The noise had roused Michaela's parents, and the voice stopped as they hurried up the stairs. The padre quickly put away the mallet and rushed for the door. He stood in the way, preventing Fiona and Buck from seeing what he'd done to their little girl.

"You must trust in the way of the Lord," he told them, close to tears himself. "Christ went through this pain to be absolved of the world's sins, and Michaela must serve penance. Pain will out the demon, so says the Lord."

The parents nodded as if they understood. Fiona gave a gasp in the doorway, and her eyes widened to a spot behind the padre for a moment. Startled, the old man looked around to the corner of the room beyond the bed. It was the place Michaela had faced when she recorded her video. Now, it was just a corner of a room, a poster of a country music concert peeling slowly from the wall.

"I'm sorry," Fiona mumbled. "I thought I saw...it must have been a shadow, is all."

"Can we see her now?" Buck asked, lips trembling.

"Of course," the padre said with a nod, "but remember, you must try not to be alarmed."

When Fiona Haverford saw what had been done to her only child, her scream carried for miles.

****

Little Jimmy Heck heard the scream that night. He was outside the back of the old farmhouse, dragging a heavy body into a deep ditch. It seemed a shame to send Elias to the grave without ceremony, so Jimmy had let him keep his whiskey bottle clasped in his firm, dead grip. Uncovering the body from the blanket had been the worst moment, and Jimmy had thrown up on the living room floor. Everything afterwards became easier somehow, like he'd managed to switch off the part of his brain that knew how to cry and feel and fear.

"That is one mighty fine grave, if I do say so myself," said Jesse.

He had arrived from nowhere, just as before, moments after the scream cut the night air. Jimmy observed the pale figure carefully, noting that his clothes were just the same as they'd been in the daytime.

"I got started as soon as school was done," Jimmy explained. "Miss Dupree gave me the part for the play today."

"Oh yeah?" Jesse said, grinning in the moonlight. "Tell me all about it, kiddo."

"It's you," Jimmy replied. He straightened up the body in the grave with a heave, then climbed out into the dark, cool evening. "I hadn't ever heard the story of Pale Jesse 'til now. The other kids all knew it, they do it every year. But Miss Dupree told me about the knife and the lasso and the horse called Mindy."

"Mindy?" Jesse asked. "I ain't never had no horse called Mindy. Mine was Thunder."

"Huh," Jimmy mused. He'd started to shovel dirt from the mound back into the grave. "I guess that got changed along the way. Anyhow, I figured it must be you. A ghost called Jesse visiting me. And you are mighty pale."

"How do you figure I'm a ghost?" Jesse inquired.

Little Jimmy chuckled at that. It was a stupid question, he thought. "You walk through walls, and you said you spoke to my mom," he reasoned. "You have to be dead."

"Nu-uh," Jesse insisted.

Jimmy stopped heaving dirt for a moment, and leaned on his spade to catch his breath. He considered the tall, slim figure before him, still equipped with his legendary weapons. Jesse raised a finger like an old storyteller, and then pointed to his chest. Jimmy couldn't help his eyes wandering over those bullet holes again. He wanted to know what it felt like to be shot to death, to know how his mother had felt in those last moments of her life.

"I'm in waiting," Jesse explained. "I'm about ready to come back to the world, and I need you to help me get there."

"Come back?" Jimmy asked. All thoughts of filling the grave were forgotten. The spade dropped with a thud. "You're saying the dead can return? You're saying my mom could come back to me?"

Jesse sucked his teeth for a moment, the sound shrill as nails on a chalkboard.

"We'll work on that once you got me done," he offered. "'Scuse me for not shaking hands on it, but I can't...well, you know."

Little Jimmy observed the cowboy's hands. They looked ordinary enough, but there was some chill in the air around Jesse that made Jimmy want to keep his distance. He hoped when he met his mother's ghost, he wouldn't feel that way about her.

"So, what do I do to help you?" Jimmy asked, fuelled by hope.

"I got me a body waiting, for this old spirit of mine to take over," he revealed, "but we've got an invocation to do. I can't get in without the right ceremony. You with me so far?"

He wasn't, not entirely, but Little Jimmy nodded all the same.

"So I need you to collect my bones," Pale Jesse continued. "I've been travelling all over this town, and I know now where they're all hid. Different places, scattered so's I couldn't collect 'em all. Old Injun magic or suchlike. I'll tell you where to dig, and you gather 'em all up. And like I promised, you can keep anything else that you find."

More digging. It wasn't the ideal job; Jimmy already hated the labor after only one night, but the thought of reuniting with his mother made him nod again. He didn't want to be alone in the world.

"Did your teacher give you a speech to learn for that play?" Jesse asked.

"She sure did," Jimmy answered brightly. "I've got to learn it by Friday next."

"No you don't," Jesse said with another whispered chuckle. "I've got a new text for you, son. The rites of the invocation. When it comes your time to speak on that stage, with the whole town watching, you're gonna speak the words to bring me back to life. Ain't that somethin'?"

Jesse's voice brightened with every sentence. Jimmy felt brighter too, starting to understand how things would work.

"And then my mom?" the little boy urged. "And then we get her bones from New York, right?"

"That's for after," Jesse replied. "You just remind me as soon as I'm in that new body."

"Yes Sir, I will Sir," Jimmy said proudly.

It was time to finish burying Elias. Pale Jesse vanished on the next breeze, and Jimmy knew he'd be back in the morning with instructions. The little boy had the whole weekend ahead of him to travel and dig for bones more than a century old. If someone as long gone as Pale Jesse could return, then Jimmy's mother would be easy to resurrect by comparison. There was only one thing that bothered Jimmy about the whole matter, and that was the body that Jesse mentioned.

Who was it that Jesse would move his spirit into? And did that meant that Jimmy's mother had to have a new body too? It was something the boy needed to consider. He was smart, perhaps too smart for his young, naïve spirit. If Jesse had a body to climb into, then Jimmy would have to get one too.

****

Michaela needed fresh nails every day. Buck told the padre the girl had made a sort of whimper when he took the old nails out on Saturday evening. The holy man said that was progress, a sign of the demon coming out by exhalation. In truth, the padre had no idea if that was right. He hadn't been able to contact the old preacher again who'd given him the exorcism method in the first place. He was beginning to think that old timer had died, and perhaps that served him right.

Burt had been able to give the padre twenty-three nails in all, which he found by scrounging behind counters and such in the old workshop at the back of his hardware store. This meant that when the minister came to the Haverfords' home on Thursday night, he was one nail short of the full ceremony. He didn't want to have to explain the deficit to the family, but there was no option. The treatment could not continue without more supplies.

"And why would I want it to continue?" Fiona Haverford screamed.

She had barely spoken two words to the padre all the week long, but now she was loquacious in her fury.

"Tell me why!" she demanded. "If she does come out of this possession, she's gonna die of septicemia instead! All those holes in her hands and her poor feet. Open wounds and blood everywhere!"

"Fiona, I understand that you're-"

"No, you don't!" she screamed, cutting him off. "How *dare* you say that you understand? Do you know what's it been like all week, having to play it like nothing's wrong? Telling people Michaela's just under the weather! I have no one to talk to! No one understands this."

Fiona's words seemed to wound her husband. The padre spotted his wince, and tried to offer him a look of temperance.

"Fiona, you love for your child-" the padre tried again.

"You know nothing about my love for my child!" Fiona spat back at once. "It's greater than my love for *your* God, I tell you that!"

Buck took in a deep breath. He tried to put his hands on his wife's bony shoulders, but she shook him off. Fiona walked to the corner of the living room where her body convulsed with sobs.

"Darlin', we have to keep the faith," Buck pressed. "This is our test, to see Michaela through the valley."

Gingerly, Buck Haverford reached into the pocket of his hunting jacket. He had five rusty nails in the palm of his hand when it emerged again. Over her shoulder, Fiona watched her husband give those nails to the padre. The holy man had a feeling she would never forgive either of them for what they had consented and agreed to. The treatment would go on, and Michaela would remain silent as the grave while her flesh was purged by ageing iron.

While Michaela's trial went on, Little Jimmy Heck had quite the adventure. He had been to places in Kitchener town that Old Elias never would have let him visit, like the bars at the far end of the road and the abattoir where Chuckie Matthews slaughtered cattle. Everywhere he went, he dug in the spot that Pale Jesse had pointed out, and he found bone after bone. They were scattered in groups, a full skeleton more or less by the time Thursday night came around, and Pale Jesse said that a few shards missing wouldn't matter. They had everything they needed to raise the old cowboy from his spirit state.

Little Jimmy had also learned his speech for the invocation. The words were funny, arranged in a grammar he didn't fully understand, and they had given him no clues as to whose body it was that Jesse would take over. But that hadn't stopped him from getting a body of his own. He hadn't told Jesse about it, though perhaps the all-seeing ghost already knew. Jimmy had been keeping his mother's vessel fresh in the old barn since the end of school on Thursday.

It was dark when Jimmy returned to the barn with the final bones. He put them in a sack alongside the others, which were stored on the seat of the old tractor he'd been tinkering with before Elias died. Jimmy peered into the sack, his bright young eyes delighted by the view. Things were coming together, and Jesse had been right about everything so far. It was good to have a purpose, and even better to know his job would have such exciting rewards.

"Jimmy," a small voice pleaded. "Jimmy, you have to let me go now."

Jimmy turned in the darkness and looked at the slim figure who was tied to the ladder which led to the shelf. She rested her head against the ladder, and Jimmy saw a trickle of dried blood stuck to that side of her face. He hadn't meant to hit her so hard when he knocked her out with a wrench; he had underestimated his strength. Now, the young woman looked weaker than ever as she pleaded in a croaky, pained tone. And Little Jimmy Heck felt strong.

"Jimmy, you've had your prank," the woman said, "but it's done now. People will wonder where I am if I don't come home."

"What people?" Jimmy asked brightly. "You don't have a husband. You live alone. That's what you told us in class."

Miss Dupree gave a sad, empty laugh. "And there was me thinking my students didn't listen."

"Besides, I can't let you go," Jimmy continued, "I need you. You're gonna be my mom."

"Oh honey," Miss Dupree said, caring to a fault, "this isn't how you get a new mom."

"No, I don't want a new one," Jimmy tried to explain. "You're gonna *be* her. Jesse's got it all figured it."

"Jesse?" Miss Dupree repeated. "You don't mean..."

"Oh yeah, he means it," Jesse replied.

Miss Dupree didn't seem to hear him, she just trailed off into wordlessness, studying Jimmy with tired but terrified eyes. Jimmy looked to where Jesse had walked through the barn wall. The cowboy stood appraising Jimmy's prisoner, sucking his teeth in thought.

"Come on, Little Jim," the pale cowboy crooned. "Let me show you what I used to do to my houseguests. Grab a scythe from over yonder, and a good, thick rope."

****

Miss Dupree was not present on the day of the Kitchener School play. The other teachers put it down to poor preparation and abandonment in times of stress. They simply hollered "The show must go on!" and fought for supremacy over who would take over. They gave Little Jimmy all sorts of instructions about how to change his speech, and he nodded and smiled and told them all he would take their advice. There was only one speech he was interested in, and he knew the words by heart. Soon, he hoped he'd use the invocation again, those same words bringing his mother into the body of Miss Dupree. She'd make a good new vessel for Mom. A fresh start. It was exactly what they both needed.

In the backstage mirror at the elementary school, Jimmy admired his costume. He wore leather chaps over old work trousers, and boots that were far less scuffed than Jesse's own. His shirt was a similar pattern, for the boy had chosen it himself from the drama department's wardrobe, and much to the wardrobe mistress's distress, Jimmy had stabbed lots of little bullet holes into it. On his head he wore a cowboy hat – which he had never seen Jesse don, but the teachers had all insisted he had to wear it – and at his waist there was a replica of the long, curved knife.

In his young hands, Jimmy held a rope. It was the one which had been around Miss Dupree's neck not twenty-four hours earlier. Jimmy held onto it, trying to remember that it was all going to be worth it. Soon, Pale Jesse would be made flesh, and he'd look after Jimmy until they got his mother back too. Perhaps he'd even stick around after that, and be some kind of father. Elias was the closest Jimmy ever had to that, and he'd only been concerned with his wife and dying. So far, Jesse's sole concern had been Jimmy, and that was something to hang onto.

"Well, don't you look just like me," Jesse surmised.

They were alone, and Jesse's ghost had no reflection in the mirror, yet Jimmy could see him standing right beside him. The little cowboy tipped his hat and Jesse gave a chuckle.

"You know what to say and when to say it?" Jesse asked.

"Yes Sir," Jimmy answered.

"And what about the bones?"

"I laid 'em out on the stage, just like you said," Jimmy told him. "Mr. Foster said they were mighty fine set dressing. He said they looked realistic."

"Idjut," Jesse said, rolling his eyes. "Come on then, son. Do your thing. I'll be waiting for you after."

When the tall cowboy vanished, Jimmy ran through his speech in his mind once more. He only got a few sentences in before there was a kerfuffle, and the little boy rushed towards the sound of a panicked teacher. It was Mr. Foster, who had finally won out as replacement director for Miss Dupree, and the hefty history teacher was flapping his arms like a wild bird.

"Oh, it's terrible!" he hollered, calling everyone close. "Burt from the hardware store just found Shelley Dupree in the Heck's barn. She's dead! She's cut up like old Pale Jesse woulda done, strangle-marks on her neck and a face-wide smile cut in."

In his terror, Mr. Foster had forgotten he was addressing children. The other kids in the play began to cry, and Jimmy watched their sadness with interest. Something hurt inside his chest to see them so sad, perhaps because he knew it was his doing. He had taken their beloved teacher away, but if they understood how badly he needed his mother, then surely they would understand. He thought about telling them, about trying to explain. But Jimmy *had* killed a person, whatever the reasoning, and he thought Mr. Foster might take him to be arrested if he spoke up now.

He couldn't afford to be locked away, not before he'd given his speech.

"Listen," said another teacher, a female with a worried look. "I didn't want to say anythin' before, but Fiona Haverford told me somethin' in confidence a few days ago. She said little Michaela ain't sick: she's possessed. The girl screamed something about Pale Jesse, and now she's touched by the Devil."

Murmurs went up in the crowd and Little Jimmy felt something change in the air. It felt heavy all of a sudden and he watched as fear flitted from one adult's face to the other. It was quickly followed by widening gazes of insanity as they grouped together.

"It musta been her!" Mr. Foster decreed. "Holy Hell, we gotta get over to the Haverfords' place. God only knows what else she might do if somebody don't stop her!"

People stampeded everywhere at once screaming and hollering about the devil in their town, acting like Little Jimmy had never seen them before. He tried to ask about the play, but nobody seemed interested in answering his questions any more. Everyone was up in arms about Michaela Haverford and Miss Dupree, and nobody would listen to the little boy dressed as Pale Jesse. In less than ten minutes, Kitchener School had emptied of nearly all its patrons. Some formed a mob to march on the Haverfords. Others simply took their children home to hide from the girl with the demon inside her.

Little Jimmy walked out onto the stage among the bones of Pale Jesse. He was alone against the dusty backdrop and the cardboard cacti, and he heaved out a sigh.

"What's wrong, young man?" asked an aged voice.

"Oh, it's you padre," Little Jimmy said sadly. "How do you do?"

He tipped his hat. The padre's lined face almost broke a smile, but something was holding back his mirth.

"Do you know where everyone's going?" the holy man asked the boy. "I tried to ask, but they were in such a hurry that no one would tell me."

Jimmy thought for a moment about his answer. "The play's cancelled, I guess," he said. "Miss Dupree's gone."

"And they're looking for her," the padre concluded, "I see."

Little Jimmy reasoned he hadn't actually lied. The old preacher had merely made up the rest of the story for himself. Jimmy didn't like the idea of lying to a holy man, but he knew he still had work to do.

"Say, do you mind if I give my speech?" the little boy asked. "I learned it all and I didn't get to perform it."

"Oh," the padre said with a little sigh. "Well, of course. You go right ahead, my child."

The padre sat down in the empty auditorium, about half-way back in the empty rows. Little Jimmy walked about the stage for a moment, hands on his hips like a cowboy, then he looked around at the bones he'd laid out. He was supposed to stand right in their centre, and make sure that his eyes had glanced over every one.

"Pale Jesse rises from the ashes tonight," Jimmy began.

His voice was quiet at first, so quiet that the padre's aged ears could barely understand his words, but it grew in volume with every sentence.

"The Old Ones decreed that he should never move about on this earthly plane again, yet Jesse shall rise and be whole. The Old Ones decreed that his bones should never meet, yet here they meet upon this ground! May the spirit of Pale Jesse take strength from these bones! May the Old Ones' curse be shattered!"

"Jimmy!" the padre called at once. "Jimmy, no! What are you saying?"

"May Jesse take the vessel who has known pain!"

"JIMMY! STOP THAT NOW!"

"May Pale Jessie rise into the flesh of the chosen!"

"JIMMY!"

"Raise him! Raise him! RAISE HIM!"

****

In that moment, Michaela Haverford's eyes cleared of their blackness.

Michaela tried to sit up in her bed, but there was a sudden, terrible pain in her hands and feet. She felt the sting of open wounds as they moved in the night air, and she looked to and fro to see the carnage that had been done while she was away. The little girl began to cry at once, and the sound woke her parents. Fiona and Buck had fallen asleep on chairs beside her bed, leaning on one another. Reunited by their hopeless grief, the mother and father awoke to the strange sound slowly. Fiona was the first to understand what was happening.

"No..." she whispered. "Yes. I mean, oh praise God! Praise him! Bucky! Bucky wake up, she's here! Our Michaela is here!"

Buck came to his senses seconds later. He put his hand to Michaela's brow, thrilled to find her warm to the touch once more. The teenager sobbed at her agony and Buck's eyes watered at the sight.

"I'm sorry," he said at once. "I'm sorry, baby girl, but we had to do this to get you better."

"You were sick," Fiona added, "so very sick, honey, But you're better now and we'll get those nasty nails out and fix you up."

"My feet, Momma," Michaela pleaded. "My feet hurt so bad!"

"I know, I know," Fiona soothed. "We'll get 'em. We'll get 'em now and get you to a doctor."

The loving mother had barely begun to lift away the patchwork blanket when the sound of fists pounded the door downstairs accompanied by angry yells and demands to be let in. Neither parent moved, terrified to have their child's secret discovered. Fiona had been worrying something like this might happen. In her weakest moment, the day before she exploded at the padre, she had told one person about Michaela's possession. She'd thought that person was worthy of her trust, but now it seemed she was wrong.

"Ignore it," Buck warned in a breathy tone, worried why the town had suddenly risen up against them. Fear threatened to take him, but he focused on his daughter. "Just keep quiet, and maybe they'll go."

The door creaked, then crunched as a horde of people smashed it down. Buck tried to race to the door to barricade it, but no sooner than he had put his body across the frame, the mob charged into the room. Buck was trapped behind the solid wood of the door, one arm visible as he flailed for aid. Fiona screamed, her eyes darting between her husband's peril and her daughter's panic. The mob was full of people she knew: schoolteachers, clerks and housewives, yet they were all contorted into a mass of wild rage. They looked nothing like themselves, and each one of them was armed with something sharp.

"Stop it!" Fiona demanded. "What the hell are you doing in my house? My daughter's sick, you've got to leave her be!"

"Oh, we know *all* about your daughter," said a man at the front, sounding crazed. Fiona recognized him as Mr. Foster, who had once been Fiona's teacher at the elementary school. "And we're here to make sure that demon can't kill again."

Fiona didn't understand. She tried to protest and push against the mob, but there were just too many of them to take on. She was crushed between and beneath their bodies as they advanced on the bed, where Michaela was still captive by virtue of the nails and ropes. The little girl gave an ear-piercing scream, tears streaked all over her face. Her eyes were as blue as oceans, and the sight of her gave many of the crowd pause. Mr Foster gave a fearful snarl and turned to address them.

"Don't be fooled!" he urged the mob. "This is the demon. We must destroy it before it kills us all."

"I..." Michaela began. The crowd fell silent, watching the sobbing child as she tried to speak. "Is this about Pale Jesse?"

If she had not mentioned his name, she might have lived. But Pale Jesse was in the mind of every child who'd been raised in Kitchener in the last hundred and fifty years. They all knew to fear him, as one knows to fear heights and darkness. The mob acted on instinct, and once the first blow was dealt, they were unstoppable. It was fortunate that neither Fiona nor Buck Haverford survived to witness their daughter's brutal death or hear her screams with every blow struck. Buck was already suffocating, his lungs crushed by the weight of the door pressed against him by the mob. Fiona had been struck on the head when she was trampled, and her internal bleeding would soon see her leave the earthly plane.

The Haverford's died on the day that Pale Jesse rose, and they were a suitable distraction.

****

"Jimmy? Are you all right, son?" asked the padre.

Jimmy sat on the edge of the stage, little legs swinging in his leather chaps. The old holy man had walked up the aisle between the seats, and come to stand before Jimmy. The raised stage put them eye to eye, and the boy looked into the padre's wrinkled gaze. He had blue eyes, clear as crystal, and they were sparkling. He didn't look panicked and terrified like he was before. Now, he was calm and patient.

"I think he's gone, padre," Jimmy answered with a sniffle.

"Who's gone, son?" the holy man replied.

"Pale Jesse," Jimmy confessed. "He said he'd come get me once the invocation was done, but now I've done it and he's not here. Maybe he didn't make it into the vessel, or maybe he's just gone on without me."

"Everybody leaves you behind, don't they Jimmy?" the padre asked. "Your mother, Martha and Elias Heck, and now the demons from the other world have abandoned you. You don't even have the Devil for a friend."

"No Sir, I don't," Jimmy agreed.

Tears fell, staining his poor little face. Jimmy was still clutching the rope lasso, but it felt hot and dirty in his grip. He threw it across the stage where it collided with the old bones, and Jimmy scratched at his palms where it had made them itchy. He could not satisfy the burning deep in the centre of each palm. Slowly, he began to sense the same pain in his feet.

"I've done bad things," Jimmy cried, "Worse than my mom ever did."

"Shh, hush now," the padre offered. "Christ was crucified for our sins. If you repent and work hard for the Lord, he'll forgive you one day."

"Really?" Jimmy asked. "Even if it was me that killed Miss Dupree? Even if I let Pale Jesse get a new body?"

"Even if," the padre replied.

He didn't seem disturbed that Jimmy had killed Miss Dupree, and Jimmy decided that must have been a preacher thing. Perhaps the padre was used to hearing all sorts of terrible things that people had done. The old man put a hand on Jimmy's shoulder, and even through the cloth he could feel the padre was cold as ice. Jimmy's hands and feet throbbed with an unstoppable agony, and he twitched and jerked as he continued to sob.

"I'm in pain, padre," he whimpered. "I don't understand what happened. Why doesn't Jesse come to tell me what to do next?"

"Because he's not your friend," the padre explained. "He used you to get what he wanted. He was never going to bring your mother back from the grave."

"How did you know that's what I wanted?" Jimmy asked in amazement.

"Isn't it what every orphan wants?" the padre reasoned.

Jimmy nodded. He curled himself into a ball on the stage, shaking and twitching. The padre rested a cold hand on the boy's hot brow for a moment, then he shook his head and sighed. The old man began to walk away slowly, up the aisle of the abandoned auditorium. Kitchener town would never be the same after the events of that night. Many would be driven to madness after the deaths of the Haverford's, and Jimmy would be taken back to the foster agency, and then onto a specialized facility, after he told them what he'd done. Everything would take care of itself, a town buried by secrets.

And the padre would leave, unable to cope with it all. And no one would question that. The padre smiled, his old face crinkling with the effort.

That was the moment the rope settled around his neck.

"Do you think I'm an idiot?" Little Jimmy inquired.

The old man was weak, and Jimmy kicked him to the ground as he pulled the rope tighter round the preacher's neck.

"You couldn't know about my mom," Jimmy seethed, furious. "I told no one but Jesse. And you'd care about Miss Dupree. You'd cry, padre, I know you would."

The padre bared his teeth, and the truth of him came through.

"Little rat bastard," Pale Jesse spluttered through the padre's old lips. "You weren't supposed to understand. The padre went through the pain of harming the child. He was the one. Let me outta-"

"No way," Jimmy replied coolly. "I understand now, about how you were gonna leave me. I can't let you do that, Jesse. You're all wrong. I see that now."

Jimmy pulled the rope tighter, and the old man struggled against the bond. Despite the demon and the cowboy spirit that now lived within the minister's body, there was something even stronger in that little boy, an evil Pale Jesse had only ever seen one other place: himself. And Jimmy was strong from all the wrenching he'd done on that old tractor. He'd proved his strength when he knocked out Miss Dupree, and later when he'd strangled her to death, but it wasn't just physical strength. That boy had a touch of darkness in him and Pale Jesse had let it out.

"You made a mistake, Pale Jesse," Jimmy revealed, "when you taught me how to kill like you did. You need to go back to being dead now, son. I'm going to fix that for you."

He yanked on the rope, holding fast until long after the padre took his last breath. Little Jimmy Heck turned the preacher on his back, and took the curved knife from the belt of his costume. It was a pretty good replica, and he'd sharpened it himself the day before to make the blade more authentic. It'd do just fine to carve a smile with.

There, in the shadows of the old auditorium, the new Pale Jesse made his mark. In years to come, he would be the legend the people of Kitchener feared most.

Strangers

It was Friday at 9pm and Valarie Bloom was getting ready to close her little bakery, standing right behind the door with her hand on the cheap open/closed sign so she could finally reverse it for the night. But right when she was in the process of flipping the sign's proclamation, the door began to open right on top of her. She quickly jumped back with a start as she saw a man's head poke through the door.

Seeing Valarie he apologetically stuttered, "Oh! I'm sorry are you closing?"

Opening the door enough to see the man that was in her doorway Valerie glanced at the diminutive form of a man as he adjusted his glasses to look at her. Squinting through the dim lighting of the shop he again offered, "I'm sorry; I didn't know you were closed."

Valerie found herself staring at the man, it wasn't that he was particularly handsome, he was actually fairly plain looking, it was the intensity she sensed just underneath the placid surface of his glasses and crew cut that made her want to learn more.

And although she was always a stickler for her schedule—it was already 5 minutes past 9—she found herself turning that sign back to "open" and telling the man, "Oh no. You're fine. Come right in!" Valarie took her place again behind her counter to see what could possibly bring this strange man to her bakery after 9 o'clock on a Friday night.

The man immediately zeroed in on a box of two dozen bright pink cupcakes and announced to Valerie, "There, that works! I'll take all of them."

Valerie reached behind the counter and pulled out all two dozen cupcakes. She boxed up the visitor's prize and rang it up on her cash register. As the man handed her some cash for the baked goods her curiosity got the best of her as she joked, "You must like pink cupcakes, are you going to a party?"

The man shook his head and informed her, "No ma'am. I'm taking these with me to the hospital tomorrow."

Valarie's brow creased in concern as she asked, "Hospital?"

He nodded. "Yes as part of my recent assignment I've agreed to a book signing in the oncology wing of the local hospital."

Staring in bewilderment Valarie echoed, "Recent assignment?"

He laughed and exclaimed, "I'm sorry! I'm talking in riddles again!" He smiled and added, "Please excuse me. I think I've been writing books for so long I forgot how to actually interact with human beings."

There was something charming about his self-deprecation that made Valerie feel at ease. The man gave her a good natured smile as he said, "Please allow me to start all over again." He extended his hand to shake and informed her, "My name is Jacob Jonas." Accepting his outstretched hand as if it were a lifeline to new and exciting reality apart from her boring day to day Minnesotan existence, Valerie felt a warm kinship as she gazed into the man's eyes. Jacob gently let her hand go as he continued. "I work for the Minnesota Herald back in St. Paul and I recently wrote a book on the rampant lead poisoning that they've discovered in the waters here."

Valarie had heard some of the reports of people getting sick in the area, it seemed like a terrible thing. People were fine one day and then were practically dropping dead the next from just drinking a cup of water. It was awful.

"Yes, it's been terrible. A little girl not far from here passed away just the other day; her poor mother was in here a few hours ago ordering refreshments for the funeral."

Jacob suddenly reached in his backpack and pulled out a copy of a book and excitedly put it down on the counter. "Here! You should read my book. It's all in there. This town has been suffering at the hands of corporate scumbags for way too long! I'm going to get to the bottom of this!" He glanced down at the box of cupcakes that he was carrying as if he had almost forgotten about them completely as he asked, "Um, how much are these again?"

* * * * * * *

Valerie was not usually the impulsive type—and was definitely not in the habit of bringing random men she had just met home—but something about this out of town stranger made her want to know more.

"I uh, I never do this," she said nervously after he'd paid for the cupcakes and still hadn't left her bakery. "But would you like to come back to my place for coffee?"

Jacob's eyes narrowed even as his lips curled into a smile. "Coffee?"

"You don't have to," she mumbled quickly. What was it about this man? She couldn't stop staring at him and the thought of him not coming home with her made her chest ache.

He reached across the counter, picked up her hand, and kissed the back of it. "I'd love to go with you, Valerie."

Her eyes lit up and she giggled like a little girl before calming herself back down. She told him she just needed to close u the bakery then they could head to her place. She wondered vaguely if she even had coffee and how messy her room was. She had a feeling things would progress to that point with this man.

Just the thought of him coming home with her filled her with joy. She had been depressed lately; a single mother of an often out of control daughter, her life seemed to be a monotonous burden of disappointment.

And as she pulled up to her house and saw the unsightly white work van of her daughter's latest dead beat boyfriend in the driveway, her heart sank once again.

Turning to Jacob she asked him, "I'm sorry Jacob but could you please take a rain check on my invitation?"

With a look of surprise Jacob intoned, "What? What do you mean? What's wrong?" Valarie glanced back toward the van parked in her driveway, and following her eyes Jacob inquired, "Who is that?"

Valerie sighed heavily as she said, "Oh that? That is just my daughter's latest in a long line of rejects, losers, and lowlifes."

Her words caused Jacob to laugh as he said, "Wow, ok, how about we just call that the R.L.L. club for short?" His humor worked well to assuage and take the sting out her anxiety and Valerie couldn't help but laugh herself.

"Cute! I like it!" She put her hand on the shifter as if she was going to put it in park but hesitated.

"Valarie, what's the matter? This is your house you shouldn't let anyone keep you from your own home."

Valarie gave Jacob a look of embarrassment as she suggested, "But what if they're—" She let her sentence trail off into uncertainty but her shameful expression and desperate pause filled in enough blanks to let Jacob know what she was worried about—walking in on her daughter and her new Romeo.

Jacob couldn't stand the fear that Valerie seemed to be living in and sought to cure her of it as he put his hand on hers and shifted the car into park as he told her, "Come on Valerie, show me your house. That's why I came here with you."

They got out of the car and went to the door where Valerie began to knock until Jacob put his hand on her shoulder. "Valerie, this is *your house*. You shouldn't have to knock."

Valerie sputtered, "I know—I know but—"

Jacob frowned. "But nothing—" He turned the knob and with the door effortlessly opening for him declared, "Look it's not even locked. Door is open!" He motioned for her to go in front of him. "Ladies first!"

Valarie took a deep breath, prepared herself for what might lay in store for her, and crossed over the threshold of her house. As Jacob shut the door behind them, everything seemed pretty quiet, but standing in the middle of the living room, Valerie began to smell something, a strong pungent kind of odor. Jacob noticed it too as he sniffed the air with a grimace.

"Is that what I think it is?"

Valerie cursed. "Yes, damn it! Cassie's been smoking pot again!"

As if in response to the accusation the two heard the loud creaking of the basement door. Valerie motioned for Jacob to follow as they went to the sound of the disturbance just in time to see Valerie's daughter Cassie arm in arm with her boyfriend. The two stumbled forward looking straight ahead, not even seeing the curious onlookers of Valerie and Jacob at their side.

The boyfriend lurched a bit unsteadily as Cassie giggled, "Marcus you dick! If you can't handle your booze, don't drink!"

They were happily oblivious but Valerie had had enough. "Cassie!"

Her daughter finally turned and caught sight of Valerie and Jacob. She stared at Jacob in surprise as her boyfriend Marcus laughed, "What is it Cass? Your mom has a boyfriend now?"

Livid Valerie stepped in front of the delinquent duo. "I want both of you out of this house right now!"

Cassie shot back angrily, "Why so you can have it all to yourself with your new guy friend! I don't think so!"

Jacob scoffed. "Oh come on."

Valerie, angered by the blatant disrespect shown to her right in front of her guest, screamed at them. "Get out of my house! Now!"

The disheveled Marcus finally sobered up a bit and told Cassie, "I'll warm up the van babe." Marcus walked to the door, but right as he was about to go out stopped and turned to Jacob, giving him a dirty look as he warned, "You better watch yourself buddy."

Jacob's eyes widened at the threat. "What? Really?"

Marcus went on out to his van, and after giving Valerie and Jacob another round of deadly looks, Cassie followed slamming the door behind her. Valerie walked over to the window to watch her daughter pile into her boyfriend's van. Already full of regret and sadness she watched as the van pulled out of the driveway. As the tires squealed sending the vehicle hurtling down the street she burst into tears. Feeling immensely sorry for the poor woman, Jacob put his arms around her as she wept.

It really wasn't like Valerie to let a man stay with her so soon after first meeting him, but after the drama with her daughter she felt emotionally paralyzed and needed the comfort Jacob was willing to provide like a drug. But even so, Jacob wasn't a 24 hour Dr. Feel Good, and as much as he felt sorry for the disheveled forty-five year old lady that had fallen into his arms, he had things to do, and people to see, he would soon be expected to deliver his findings as well as engage in a book signing at the cancer wing of the hospital. He could stay the night to help her get through this emotional time, but then he had to leave her.

Nothing could deter him from his goals, so he had Valerie drop him off at his hotel the next morning. Back in his room he quickly snatched up his nicely pressed, dry-cleaned suit that was still hanging in the plastic and hit the shower. About fifteen minutes later he was ready to go, grabbing his briefcase he sat down at the desk checking his notes. He knew that in order to prove his case about the contamination his presentation against the city's water management had to be perfect. Suddenly feeling the weight of responsibility on his shoulders for what he was about to do, he put the documents back in their place and slammed the briefcase shut and headed out the door before he lost his nerve.

It was as his back was turned locking his hotel room that he felt a cold piece of metal jabbing him in the back, followed by a man's voice telling him, "You make a sound, one fucking sound, and you're dead." The man grabbed Jacob's arm and spun him around bringing into his vision a man whose head was covered in a toboggan style mask. Jacob was herded into the back of a worn out, white work van. Jacob stared in terror as the morning sunlight cut off into darkness as the van's doors slammed behind him.

****

Back in her house, sitting alone at the kitchen table Valerie once again felt herself collapsing into self-despair and doubt. Was she a horrible mother? Kicking her daughter out of the house? Cassie was twenty-four years old and certainly old enough to take care of herself but still—she couldn't help but feel guilty for the way things had turned out. If only she hadn't been so emotional, she kept telling herself, if only she had tried to remain calm, maybe none of this would have happened.

She couldn't take it anymore, beating herself up like this, and she knew that the best way to get out of this slump was to take some action. So taking a deep breath she picked up her phone and dialed up Cassie. The phone rang a few times, and then right when she thought that it was about to go to voicemail she heard her daughter sullenly answer.

"What do you want now?"

Despite the biting venom in her daughter's words Valerie was immensely relived just to hear her voice. "Cassie! How are you? I just wanted to make sure were alright."

Cassie snapped back. "What the fuck? What do you mean am I alright? You just kicked me out of the fucking house!"

Feeling her blood begin to boil already, Valerie sighed heavily as she pleaded, "Cassie please. Don't use that language."

"Fuck you bitch! I'm not in your house anymore. And newsflash! I'm a grown woman, I can say whatever the fuck I want!"

Fighting back tears Valerie said, "Cassie….I know you're grown….but can't you at least spare your poor mother's feelings and not talk like that—"

Cassie didn't and screamed instead. "You kicked me out of the house! What else is there to say?"

Valerie couldn't stand to hear such words and as always buckled under the pressure. "Cassie please I was upset….you can come back whenever you want."

Cassie laughed and told her coldly, "Forget it! I'm getting off here!"

Before she hung up Valerie pleaded, "Cassie wait! Where are you? What are you doing?"

"None of your damn business," Cassie snapped and hung up the phone.

Shaking in distress, Valerie stared at the phone as her daughter disconnected from her and let it slip from her hands as she burst into tears. She was a frantic mess; she didn't know what to do, or who to call. *What about Jacob?* she thought. But he hadn't even left a phone number. *Just how pathetically desperate am I?* She let this strange man into her life and didn't even have enough sense to get his phone number?

The thought occurred to her that he was having a public book signing that afternoon at the cancer ward of the hospital; she would just go there and see him. She couldn't just drown herself in grief all alone, she needed someone to share it with, and Jacob was the most promising candidate that she had had for a while. So as much as she felt like a desperate stalker she made her way to the hospital for his book signing.

Arriving around 11:30 AM, she knew that he should have already been in the hospital. She saw the conference table set up and a crowd was already seated waiting for him, but instead of seeing any sign of Jacob she saw a couple very anxious PR guys pacing back and forth and talking amongst each other. Not sure what else to do, Valerie went ahead and took a seat with the rest of the onlookers. She noticed a young woman with a little girl sitting next to her.

The girl was waving Jacob's book in the air when she dropped it, causing it to bounce right at Valerie's feet. The mother snapped at her daughter. "Margaret! What are you doing?"

Valerie quickly grabbed the book and handed it back to the mother telling her, "Oh no. Don't worry about it. It's ok."

The woman smiled at Valerie and thanked her before asking, "Are you here to see Dr. Jacob Jonah?"

Resisting a slight twinge of embarrassment Valarie answered, "Yes, yes I am."

The three of them then sat in silence as they waited for Dr. Jacob's arrival. As they watched the two P.R. men continue to consult with themselves behind the table, a woman suddenly came rushing up to them. Valerie and the woman next to her strained to try and hear their hushed voices, as Valerie wondered out loud, "What are they saying?"

The P.R. team's discussion abruptly ended as the woman rushed back to the other room and one of the men grabbed the microphone on the table to announce to the waiting audience, "Ladies and Gentlemen, we have some terrible news." The man then paused and swallowed nervously as if the words themselves were painful to deliver as he continued, "Dr. Jonas will not be here today, he has been abducted. If anyone has any information as to his last whereabouts. Please come forward and let us know."

****

Valarie sat at the police station for about an hour before they finally called her in for questioning. The first question pierced right through her with its barely concealed accusation. "So you were the last person to see Dr. Jonas?"

Biting her lip in frustration, Valerie nervously exclaimed, "Well, no! I mean—that the last people to see him must be the ones holding him hostage!"

Detective Johnson grew impatient and snapped. "Come on Valerie, you know that's not what we mean. What we're asking here is were you the last person to see him before this incident happened?"

Valerie buried her face in her hands, not wanting to even see the overbearing detective's face as she groaned, "Yes—yes, I dropped him off at his hotel room and as far as I know I was the last person to see him before this happened."

The detective sighed and asked, "Did you see anything suspicious when you left the hotel? Any strange vehicles or anything?"

The mention of strange vehicles got her attention and creasing her brow in concern she asked, "What do you mean strange vehicles?" The police woman who had been standing nearby pulled a piece of paper out of a file and put it down on the table in front of Valerie.

She gasped in shock as she saw it was a photo printout of what appeared to be Cassie's boyfriend's white work van. The detective picked up on her anxiety and slammed his fist down on the table for emphasis to get her full attention. "What? What is it Valerie? You've seen this vehicle before?"

Valerie not knowing what to do shook her head and lied. "No-no. I've never seen anything like that."

The detective laughed gruffly. "Well from the look on your face you could have fooled me."

Valerie shook her head and with twitching hands stood from the table. "Ok, if you don't mind. I think I've answered enough questions."

The female officer put up her hand in protest. "Wait! Ma'am, I don't think you quite get the gravity of the situation, a man was found dead." She pointed at the photo of the van and added, "And you get a panicked look on your face just from seeing this photo, something just doesn't seem right here, now did you see this van before or not?"

Valerie shook her head sadly and moaned, "Please, I don't know."

Detective Johnson raised his eyebrow and asked softly, "You don't know?" He looked at Valerie very seriously and told her, "Look Valerie, this is very important, we're not trying to implicate you in this; we just want to know if you've seen this van. We aren't actively investigating you as a suspect but if we find that there is something that you are not being truthful with us about, believe me, you soon will be quite a person of interest."

Valerie nodded slowly, but didn't say anything yet.

Johnson stared intently at her and leaned forward on the table. "So I'm going to ask you again, have you seen this van?"

Valerie sighed heavily. "I told you, I don't know." She looked anxiously up at Johnson and told him, "Please, can I go now?"

Johnson frowned, but gave the female police officer a knowing look and then turned back to Valerie and told her with concealed sarcasm, "Thank you for your cooperation."

Running on autopilot, Valerie got up and quietly thanked her questioners and left the room. As soon as she shut the door, the female officer asked the Detective, "Ok Johnson? What do you think?"

Detective Johnson shook his head and replied, "You saw her reaction when we showed her the picture of that van right?" The officer nodded as he grimaced. "So she obviously knows something she's not telling us. Put a trace on her phone, I want every call she makes from here on out monitored."

And just like clockwork as soon as Valerie got in her car she dialed up her daughter. Cassie didn't pick up at first, so she frantically dialed the number again, and this time Cassie answered.

"You again? What the fuck do you want already?"

Valerie sobbed into the phone. "Cassie! Cassie! This is serious! I'm at the police station, they have pictures of your boyfriend's van. I think he's been linked to the disappearance of Jacob!"

Cassie laughed incredulously. "What the hell is this mom? Is this some kind of crazy strategy to get me back? Me and Marcus have been inseparable for the past few days. Maybe you should lay off the pot yourself!"

"Cassie! Cassie listen to me," Valerie sputtered, but the only answer she received was the hanging up of the phone. Valerie stared straight ahead in a state of shock, but while she was busy hanging up the phone, the eyes and ears that watched her from Detective Jonson's office were on full alert.

****

Detective Johnson was a man who didn't give up, and usually once he had even the slightest bit of a lead, he didn't rest until he acquired his target. It was this unrelenting drive that had him holed up in the Big Jugs Bar and Grill. The place epitomized sleaze and degradation, the manager made sure that the waitresses all wore the tightest fitting uniforms possible, their tops unbuttoned just enough to showcase the best of their "Jugs".

It only took him five minutes back in the office to run a search on Cassie Bloom to find that she worked at this dive. And it didn't take him any time at all to spot her working in the restaurant. As soon as he sat down, he saw her waiting the table across from him, where a middle aged man seemed to be chatting her ear off. She was a pretty enough girl with her long, light brown hair billowing over her shoulders, but she didn't seem to have any self-respect.

Detective Johnson cringed as he saw the customer purposefully drop his check just so he could watch her bend over to pick it up. The old man followed her down with his eyes and Detective Johnson watched the man's hands reach out as if to grab the waitress. She in turn moved even closer as if ready to let him do it. Just like he thought, no self-respect. As soon as she had finished taking care of her leering admirer, Johnson got her attention.

"Miss! Miss please! I've been here for almost a half hour and no one has waited on me!'

Cassie turned around and headed his way. With a smile she said, "Oh I'm sorry sir. What would you like?"

"Oh, just a cup of coffee—" Johnson paused as he pulled the photo of the van and handed it to Cassie, flashed her his badge, and continued, "And I would like to know whose van this is."

Cassie's pleasant demeanor turned to a defiant snarl as she slammed the picture down on the table and whispered, "I don't have to answer any damn questions. I know my rights."

Johnson smirked. "Do you? Then you might also be interested to know that you have a warrant out for your arrest." He pulled a piece of paper from inside his jacket and held it up before her eyes.

Cassie's defiant front collapsed as her lips quivered anxiously. "What? What are you talking about?"

"It seems you never made it to court on the 15th young lady. You have an outstanding drug charge and now it's found its way to warrant status."

As Cassie peered around the bar in panic to see if anyone was looking at her she begged, "Please. I don't need this right now."

Detective Johnson nodded and told her, "Ok, then take me to your boyfriend. I'd like to take a look at that van of his."

****

As planned Detective Johnson followed Cassie's car after she left work. He kept at a distance, just close enough to keep on her tail. When he saw her pulling into the rundown trailer park just off the freeway exit he couldn't help but mutter to himself, "Just as I figured..." Johnson parked at a distance and then got out of his car and walked up to Cassie in the driveway.

As Johnson approached Cassie glanced at him and said, "You better just take it easy—for your sake." With this ominous warning Detective Johnson followed Cassie to the door. Even though she had a key she went ahead and knocked.

After a few seconds of stomping could be heard through the thin mobile home siding, Marcus opened the door mumbling, "Cass, what happened to your key?" He saw Detective Johnson standing behind her, and asked him, "Who the hell are you?"

Detective Johnson presented his police badge and informed Marcus, "I want to have a look at your van."

Marcus shot a menacing look to Cassie but turned back to the Detective and complied with a shrug. "Ok officer sure thing. I've got nothing to hide." He acted as if he were about to step outside but right when he stepped forward he reached out and grabbed Cassie yanking her to himself and in an instant had a gun to her head.

"Marcus! What are you doing?" she screamed.

"Shut up bitch. That Eco-Terrorist had a price on his head! They paid me a lot of money to waste him, and now you're my extra collateral!"

Detective Johnson started to reach for his gun, not taking his eyes from Marcus, but the man saw it and pressed the barrel harder against Cassie's temple.

"Drop it right now unless you want this bitch's brains to splatter all over you! Drop it!"

In his younger days Johnson may have tried to do something brash, such as charge the deranged nutcase and wrestle the gun from his hands. But being just a few years short of retirement, all such audacious notions had left him long ago, and he just couldn't take the risk. So he quietly dropped the gun just as he was asked.

"Now turn around and put your fucking hands up asshole!" Marcus screamed.

Marcus roughly tossed Cassie away from him making her trip and fall on the ground. He charged toward Detective Johnson and putting the gun to his back ordered him to get moving. Marcus led the Detective to the back yard of the trailer sending him in the direction of what looked like a utility shed.

Detective Johnson made careful note of his location and glancing through the corner of his eyes he tried to see if there were any witnesses, but the trailer park was strangely quiet. As they stopped at the shed, Marcus jerked Detective Johnson to the side with his gun still trained on him as he struggled to open the door. Not liking the prospects of letting this low life holding him prisoner in a bug infested trailer park storage shed, Johnson saw what he thought was a chance to turn the tables.

Marcus seemed to really be struggling with the rusted lock and in his brief frustration he started to lower the gun. Johnson was just getting ready to make a move toward the weapon when his chance was blown by a sobbing Cassie rushing to them crying.

"Marcus! How could you?"

"Bitch please! I couldn't let you blow this deal for me. Now get back in the trailer," he snapped as he spun around.

Cassie wasn't having it though and as she raised her hand Detective Johnson recognized his service revolver in her shaking hands. Marcus with his gun still trained on Johnson found himself in a difficult spot, right in the crosshairs of his frantic girlfriend.

"Cass baby please. You have to understand. That guy—Dr. Jacobs he was up to no good nosing around town causing a lot of trouble. Someone from the water company wanted to shut him down, get him to stop talking. They offered me a million dollars for a job Cass. A million dollars. I couldn't pass it up."

With tears streaming down her face Cassie shouted, "You creep! You did it all for money!"

"No Cassie I did it for us! I don't want us to struggle. Your mom's always saying about how I'm a low life and I can't provide for you. I just—after this one big pay out—I could take care of you baby!"

"Liar," Cassie sobbed. "Is that what you call putting a gun to my head? Taking care of me?"

Marcus glanced at Detective Johnson and then coldly looked back at the weeping form of Cassie. He jerked his gun away from the Detective to fire upon his girlfriend. The old Detective however, finally digging deep inside himself found the reserve of strength he had left over from his better years, and prepared himself for the fight.

Right as Marcus was pulling the trigger, Detective Johnson screamed, "No!" and charged forward, tackling Marcus to the ground as he fired shots in the air. Even with this burst of energy however, the Detective struggled against a man twice his size and as he wrestled for the gun, he was soon in danger of being overpowered himself.

All of this happened in an instant, but as it sunk into Cassie's grieving heart that there was no doubt of what her lover would have done to her, anger took over and she charged forward.

With the pure rage of the jilted she dropped to her knees and put the gun right to Marcus's head as she screamed, "Drop the damn gun Marcus or I swear to God I will kill you myself!"

Marcus froze as the Detective grappled with his iron grip. He looked over to Cassie and admonished her, "I don't believe you Cass. You don't have the guts!"

Cassie cocked back the gun getting ready to fire. "Really Marcus?"

It was when he looked into her eyes in that moment that his stare of defiance turned into fear and disbelief, staring into the cold vacuum that had been his former lover. He suddenly knew this woman wouldn't hesitate to put a bullet in his brain. Marcus, knowing he was defeated, let the gun drop from his hand. And as Cassie kept the gun on him, Johnson ordered, "Ok buddy put your hands behind your back!" Marcus rolled to his stomach and offered up his two hands behind his back as Johnson slapped the cuffs on his wrist and declared, "You're under arrest for the murder of Dr. Jacob Jonas!"

****

The funeral of Dr. Jacob Jonas was a solemn affair. He had no wife, no children, and both of his parents were already deceased. But although his relatives were sparse in attendance, this was made up for by the hundreds of others who knew him through his activism, or had somehow just briefly graced his presence in this life.

People like Valerie Bloom.

She had only known the doctor for one night really, but the tragedy tore at her soul, not so much of how he had died, but more the death of what could have been. It was the possibility of a relationship with this man that had been ripped prematurely from her that felt like such a cruel trick of fate. She couldn't say she was in love with the man, but she knew she wasn't far from it, and it was the assassin's bullet that had forever taken away from her what could have been.

It was as she knelt down by his casket with tears streaming down her face that she felt a hand on her shoulder. She turned to see the equally grief stricken face of Cassie. In great emotional distress she knelt down by her mother and told her, "Mom, I am so sorry." Valerie then put her arms around her daughter, as Cassie continued to sob, "I'm so sorry."

As she held her daughter, Valerie felt the strange realization that she was going to be alright. Somehow knowing Jacob for that one night had lifted her out of her misery, a feeling she could only describe as being touched by a good soul. She voiced these feelings to her distraught daughter the best way she could, holding her tighter as she reassured her, "It's ok sweetheart. Everything is going to be ok from now on."

Camera Monstura

A few months earlier...

"Now everybody bunch up. That's it. Closer or I won't fit you all into the frame."

"I love that camera, Arch. So vintage. I used to have one like that."

"I can't wait to see the picture!"

"You won't have to, Ally. It's what they call an instamatic."

"Stop talking! Get ready to smile everyone."

"Hang on! Charlie's pushing me!"

"Three, two, one, say cheese."

"Cheese!"

****

Arch had cut the top of the Ally's head off in the photo. There just wasn't room for everyone in the frame. Granddad had lifted Charlie up so he was head-height with the others, and therefore able to shove his hand right into his sister Layla's face. Arch's mother was busy trying to calm her grandkids and look pretty for the picture at the same time. Their jostling had pushed Ally out, only her shoulders remaining visible.

When Arch was finished, she was the only one left alive.

"You have to believe me," he pleaded, his voice quaking. "I don't know what just happened. I can't remember a thing."

Ally had been sick from the shock, and the sight of her vomit made Arch want to throw up too. Blood caked his hands, almost black with its thickness. He couldn't look at himself, or see the crimson stains seeping into his bright summer shirt. The shirt would never wash clean. *He* would never wash clean.

"You monster," Ally whispered. "You just stay back you fucking monster!"

She held a kitchen knife – the one he'd used on Granddad – and her grip was firm. Ally was full of the horror she had just witnessed, and Arch believed every word and motion of her threat. She'd kill him if he tried to reach for her. She had the knife in one hand and her mobile in the other, but her fingers seemed to fumble over the touch screen.

"I want you to call the police," Arch said.

Ally paused. "You do?"

"Of course I do," her husband replied. "We need to make sense of what's gone on."

The knife wavered briefly.

"I'll tell you what's gone on," Ally sobbed. "You've killed my babies. Little Charlie and Layla, their whole futures wiped out in a heartbeat by *you* and your knives. You killed your mother Arch. *Your mother*, who loved you so much. And your poor old cheerful granddad. I saw the look in his eyes when he died. Shocked. Horrified. No one should have to die that way."

With every word she spoke, Arch felt the truth penetrate his shaking body. He could remember it all, as though he was watching a violent movie. He knew all his loved ones were dead, save for her. He knew that a summer picnic in an Essex garden had turned into a bloodbath by his own hands. But he didn't know *why*. He couldn't remember the part where he'd gone from loving father to psychotic killer and back.

"Please Ally," he pleaded once more. "I don't know how this happened. Something happened to me. Something took me over!"

He wanted her to believe him. After everything, he couldn't lose her too. But Ally found the courage to dial the emergency number, and soon the police and the coroner were on their way. When the forces arrived, Arch was sitting on the porch of his grandfather's pleasant little house. He was taken away with no resistance, tears and confusion his only expressions. Ally had been sick again and again. She'd never be the same after all she had seen.

Nobody stopped to look at the instamatic camera. The photo it had taken, which contained all of the photographer's victims, was slowly decomposing in the river of their blood.

****

Present Day

Debra Jasper hated the Piccadilly Line. All year round, the tube train was filled with tourists from every nation, most of them heading to London's famous Covent Garden. Culture, fine dining, and theatre awaited those who could afford it, and it seemed there was no short supply of ready money on the train. This also attracted beggars and thieves to the Piccadilly Line, who mingled among the standees in search of open pockets and loose zips on handbags. Debra had seen dozens of tourists get robbed blind, and she'd seen twice as many simply drop their money by mistake.

On that particular evening, Debra thought she'd seen a banknote flutter to the ground as a group of Japanese tourists were getting off the train. They'd alighted at Leicester Square, probably to pick up theatre tickets, which left Debra to reach out and pick up their leftovers. She was a little disappointed when she realized she wasn't holding money. The scrap of paper turned out to be a small, glossy photograph, similar to an instant Polaroid. Within the frame, a cheerful Japanese couple stood on London Bridge.

Debra studied their faces. The young woman was impossibly cheerful, a massive smile covering half of her face. The man, she assumed was his boyfriend, had his arms wrapped around her tiny waist, and leaned against her body full of love and affection. It made Debra feel lonely, looking at their happiness. The young man had stylish hair – streaked with silver like a cartoon character – and the pair of them wore t-shirts with nerdy slogans. A pair truly made for one another, Debra reckoned. It was a shame they had lost their photograph of such a happy moment.

Covent Garden was the next stop, and Debra alighted the train into the underground station. People flocked to and fro in unstoppable streams of motion, and it was simply a case of join a stream or face the crush. Debra managed to weave into the right lane of human traffic, following it up the escalators and out into a crisp summer evening. The streets of Covent Garden itself were little better than the closed confines of the station, and Debra had to push past the endless mass to get down onto Bow Street. She was heading for Drury Lane, where the historic Theatre Royal attracted more than two thousand people every night.

It was fortunate for Debra that she didn't have to use the main doors to enter the lavish Georgian theatre. The stage door was located on a deserted backstreet, inconspicuous save for the faded brass lettering on its old wooden façade. Inside the doorway, a guard waited behind a window, his grey face washed out with fatigue and boredom. Debra smiled at him, as she always did, and signed herself into his visitor's book.

"Busy out there tonight, Doc?" the man in the box asked.

"Heaving, Stan," Debra replied. "You'll have a crowd out here later tonight, I reckon."

"What's new?" Stan replied with a heavy shrug.

As she started up the corridor that led to the dressing rooms, Debra wondered about Stan. She couldn't help but analyze people, and Stan was difficult to place. He hated crowds, music and actors, but he worked in a theatre. Perhaps there was something about the relative peace of sitting in a tiny office that appealed to him, watching sports on his phone during the quiet periods. Or perhaps it was simply this particular job had fallen into his lap, and he was too afraid of change to go out and grab any other opportunity. In Debra's experience, most people were afraid of change until it happened. Then you could see what a real human being was made of.

"Doctor Jasper!"

Someone called Debra from the corridor ahead. She recognized the face as that of Lyle Waite, understudy for the lead of the musical that was now halfway through its season. Lyle had not yet had a chance to actually perform on the stage at Drury Lane, and judging by the terrified look on his face, it appeared his moment might have arrived at last. He waved a dark hand at Debra, worry brimming in his huge brown eyes.

"He says he won't go on," Lyle said, nodding towards the dressing room door beside him. "He's locked us all out! Its forty minutes to curtain up and he's not even in costume yet. Do something, Doctor, please! Only you can-"

Debra raised a hand, and Lyle fell silent.

"All right," she said calmly. "I'll see what I can do."

As she turned towards the door emblazoned with the legend REGGIE LEXINGTON, Debra rolled her eyes. This happened every Wednesday, and Lyle got into an unstoppable panic every Wednesday, yet every Wednesday Reggie Lexington took the stage to a standing ovation. It was Doctor Debra Jasper's considered opinion that actors simply enjoyed drama. She was practically being paid to play a role in their backstage production. She knocked on Reggie's door four times, a signature rhythm. There was a pause, just as there always was.

And then:

"Come."

And she went in.

****

The pre-show session was the working part, and it was never enjoyable to bring Reggie down from his well-rehearsed tantrum. The interval of the musical, however, was always fun. Reggie was joyous after his superb performance in the first half, and he poured sparkling wine and offered Debra platters of fresh fruit dipped in chocolate.

"Honestly, if I wasn't on stage six nights a week, I'd be fat as a hog," he remarked.

Debra liked Reggie when he was calm and collected. He had dark, wavy hair that he often ran his fingers through, and glassy eyes that were sometimes grey and sometimes green. He was handsome, witty and charming, about ten years older than Debra, pushing forty but looking fine for it. And he was gay as a maypole.

"Did you see Lyle mugging me from stage left?" Reggie asked, not waiting for an answer. "Bitch. I'll have his guts for garters if he does it again."

Debra was halfway through a particularly large strawberry, and she simply nodded her head. She hadn't seen Lyle doing anything of the sort, she had been far too immersed in the melodious musical to notice that sort of thing. Even though she had seen the show a few times before, thanks to Reggie's complimentary house seats, it still lifted her out of her dreary, lonely world for three hours a week. It was a decent perk in an otherwise rueful occupation.

"Oh, you *are* the best shrink I've ever had," Reggie said. He reached out and patted the back of Debra's hand firmly.

"I'll bet you say that to all the clinical psychiatrists," she replied dryly.

Reggie gave a bark of a laugh, flashing perfect teeth. "Darling, I mean it," he assured her. "I couldn't go back out there tonight without you."

There came a wild rapping at Reggie's dressing room door. He sighed dramatically, but before he could tell the impatient visitor to come in, the door burst open. It was Lyle who entered the room, flustered and more wide-eyed than ever. Debra had seen him worried before, but this was different, beyond his own theatrics. This was genuine fear.

"Second half's cancelled," Lyle revealed.

"Like hell it is!" Reggie exclaimed, leaping to his feet. "If this is that puffed up little director Meadows, I'll-"

"No, no, no!" Lyle cut in. "It's nothing like that. There's…" The understudy paused, gasping to catch his breath. "There's been a murder in the auditorium."

"A murder?" Debra exclaimed.

Lyle nodded gravely. "A double murder, right in front of everyone."

Reggie sank slowly into his chair. He gave a heavy sigh and shook his head. "Blast," he remarked. "I was on good form tonight too…"

****

Debra lived alone in a flat in Tooting. Her doctor's wage paid for a modest establishment south of the River Thames, and her stylish kitchen counters were so clean, she could see her face in them. Her long brown hair was lank that morning, her dark eyes lacking their luster. She felt ill, a deep psychological sense of weight settling in all her limbs. She stared at the television set perched on the corner of the counter, waiting patiently for the news. Its bell-chime theme reverberated around the empty apartment.

"Our top story this morning," the anchor began, his ageing face grave. "A tourist couple were viciously murdered in Drury Lane Theatre last night, following the crazed rampage of a fellow holidaymaker. Our correspondent Stacey King has the story."

The scene shifted. Debra had seen Stacey King around London quite often. She was the culture correspondent, working mainly in the West End, and the actors and actresses she interviewed were usually the same ones who hired Debra for psychological support. Stacey was a short girl with a bob of black hair and ruby red lips. Today, though her make-up was fully in place, she looked like death warmed up. It wasn't in her remit to report homicides, but the crime had landed in her territory.

"A young couple very much in love, enjoying a night at the theatre," Stacey began. "That was how yesterday evening began for Makoto Takahashi and Sakiko Ito, two Japanese students taking their first European holiday together. They had been to Rome, Paris, and Berlin, but it was here in London where they met a terrible fate."

Photographs scrolled onto the screen, and Debra felt her hands trembling. She *knew* that couple, and yet she couldn't possibly know them. The young woman had a smile that covered half her face, and the young man had hair streaked with silver. The photos, according to the legend beneath, were courtesy of Makoto's social media page, showing recent shots of the pair. In one picture, they were wearing the very same nerdy t-shirts that Debra had seen the day before.

It wasn't possible.

Where had she put that instant photo she found on the tube? For a moment, Debra had a terrible feeling she'd cast it away, but when she fumbled in her handbag, the picture tumbled out. She almost crushed it in her hurry to set it straight, cradling the glossy piece of paper in her palms. Debra's eyes roved over the t-shirts, and the sight of London Bridge in the background.

But the faces were gone. Sakiko's huge grin was no more; she was simply a blur of white and golden hues. Makoto's silver-streaked hair was just about visible, but his visage had swirled into a mass of black. Only their faces were blurred, nothing else in the shot, and Debra wondered whether something in her bag had leaked and spoiled those spots on the picture. When she searched her make-up and other possessions, she could find nothing damp or leaking.

The news report had moved onto something else, but Debra was not ready to let go of her revelation. She reached for her phone and searched the news, spelling the couple's names as best she could. The result came up under the headline: GRUESOME DOUBLE KILLING BY TOTAL STRANGER. Debra loaded the article, the faded photo firm in her grip. In this particular rendition of the couple's tragic story, the reporter had honed in on the identity of the murderer, who had mercifully been caught at the scene.

The killer was fellow tourist Anders Bloch, a Swedish backpacker aged twenty-seven. Bloch had absolutely no connection to either Makoto or Sakiko, and he had not purchased a ticket to attend the musical at the Theatre Royal that night. Bloch simply entered the building during intermission, approached the couple, and stabbed the woman in the neck with the knife, turned and stabbed the boyfriend in the chest before anyone could stop him. After the grisly scene, eyewitnesses report that Bloch sat down among the theatre seats in a state of shock, and he claimed he had no memory of the events which had just occurred.

A knock at the door threw Debra from her reverie. She started, her pulse thumping in her throat, and slowly moved towards her front door. The flats had one of those buzzer things downstairs to let people in, so there was never any reason for someone to be knocking directly on her door. Debra approached the dull grey paneling of the entryway, resting her ear against it just as the interloper banged again. She pulled away, wincing, but not before she heard a familiar low sigh on the other side.

"Thank God you're in," said a familiar voice as she opened the door, "but then, where else would you be? You've no life besides work, have you?"

"Tactless as always, Reggie," Debra remarked.

He was half-cut already, despite the early morning hour, and he clasped an antique-looking hip flask in one hand. The great Reggie Lexington was always dressed for a gala, and this morning his white cashmere scarf was strewn over a crocodile skin jacket. Debra could only hope that the fabric was imitation. Reggie walked wearily past the kitchen counter, settling himself on Debra's sofa instead.

"Crickey, this is rock hard," Reggie said, touching the cushions forlornly. "Do you never sit here?"

She frowned. There was no one to sit with. Debra found herself far more comfortable at the singular stool of the breakfast bar, but now Reggie was watching her expectantly. She crossed the room, picking up her phone on the way, and perched on the corner of the sofa. There was only one sure-fire way to get Reggie to stop asking her questions about her sad, lonely existence, and that was to put him back at the centre of attention.

"I take it you don't have a performance on tonight?" she asked, indicating the hip flask.

"Eighty-seven percent of the week's tickets returned," Reggie said mournfully. "I told them, I said: Reggie Lexington does not play to a near-empty house!"

"You mean, they're keeping the theatre open?" Debra asked in amazement. "Even after what just happened?"

Reggie nodded and took another swig from his flask. "They say they're duty-bound. If there are customers, then the show must go on," he continued. "And I told them to stuff it."

"And how did they take that?" Debra said.

Reggie's handsome face was drawn in, like he'd sucked a lemon. "They replaced me with that little cow Lyle," he revealed, "at least until the attendance goes back up."

And that was why Reggie was sitting in her apartment. For all the teasing he did about Debra not having a life outside of work, she knew that Reggie was just as solitary. He wouldn't be knocking on his shrink's door so early in the morning otherwise. Debra toyed with her phone, unlocking the screen to reveal the remainder of the story about Anders

Bloch. Her eyes glossed over the words again: *no memory of the events which had just occurred.*

"Have you heard anything about this Swedish bloke who did the killing?" she asked.

"Oh, him?" Reggie replied. "He's being remanded in custody in the local station, up around Theatreland."

"The local station?" Debra retorted. "I thought someone like him... someone who'd done something so brutal ought to be taken straight to a more secure place, surely?"

"Budget cuts," Reggie said with a shrug, "they can't move him until there's room. Anyway, since the incident he's been perfectly normal."

"How do you know all this?" Debra pressed.

"One of the chorus girls is going out with a police officer who works nights at that station," he said. "They go on daytime dates, isn't that charming?"

Nothing about dating seemed charming to Debra. It only made her think back to the Japanese couple and their once-happy photograph. Her eyes roved back to the breakfast bar, where that strangely faded photo sat beside the television set.

"I wonder if I could get in to see him," she mused aloud.

"See him?" Reggie replied. "What the devil for?"

It was a good question, and Debra really didn't have a convincing answer.

"Professional curiosity," she lied. "Believe it or not, we psychiatrists would much rather be studying the minds of murderers than soothing the egos of overpaid actors day in, day out."

"Overpaid, my arse!" Reggie exclaimed. "I'll bet you make more than I do."

Silence fell, and Debra's head swirled with images of Makoto and Sakiko, their faces melting into a colorless blur. Until Reggie slapped a hand on his thigh.

"Well, let's go down there and see if we can get you an interview," he suggested, as if it were that easy.

"How are we planning on doing that exactly?" she asked him.

"Darling, it's all about the presence," Reggie explained. "You've got the real credentials. All you need is the bluff. Walk in and tell them you're here to profile the Swede. It's only a local station, they won't have a clue what's hit them. And I'll back you up of course, with my superior acting talents. To action!"

When Reggie rose on his last words, his legs gave a precarious wobble. Debra frowned at him.

"Maybe a few gallons of coffee for you first?" she suggested.

"Rather, yes," Reggie conceded with a grin.

****

Anything was worth a shot to quell her curiosity about the double murder. And, to Debra's total disbelief, Reggie managed to get her a ten minute interview with Anders Bloch. Once he was sober, he'd nipped back to the theatre to find a threateningly sharp suit to wear, and he and Debra had walked into the Theatreland district as though they owned the place. A few well-placed words from Reggie, and a flash of Debra's qualifications, she found herself standing at the door to Interview Room Six. Beyond it, there was a man who'd stabbed two people so brutally fast, and suddenly Debra's curiosity gave way to abject fear.

It was far too late to back down, despite the cold gooseflesh that had overtaken her skin. Debra's heart thumped in her chest like a wild beast, and she knew deep down this was the very reason she'd taken up counseling actors instead of pursuing the criminal route. She was timid at heart, almost afraid to really get out there and live. This was the first out of character act she'd ever made, and what a way to go off the rails. The sergeant opened the door for her, and Debra stepped inside despite her every instinct.

Bloch sat at the table, looking like a man who'd lost everything. He was thin and ginger, with a slightly overgrown beard and a long face made all the longer by sadness. When he saw Debra, he looked up with empty eyes. He didn't seem dangerous, only sad to the extreme. Debra sat down opposite him at the table, and she was grateful for the sergeant, who remained in the room.

"Mr. Bloch," she began, "my name is Doctor Jasper. I'd like to ask you a few questions about your day leading up to the incident. We don't have to mention the theatre at all, just what happened before it. Is that all right?"

Bloch nodded shakily. Debra reached into her handbag for a notebook and pen. The sharp edge of the instant photo poked out of the back cover of the notebook, and Debra ran her finger over it protectively.

"Tell me what you were doing during the daytime," she urged gently.

"I was doing the tourist thing," Bloch said, his voice thick with the Swedish accent. "I wanted to see as much of London as possible. I only have a few days, before I move on to see Stonehenge."

"So where did you go?" Debra asked.

Bloch lifted one hand, and both Debra and the sergeant shifted a little. The murderer didn't seem to notice their flinching, he merely held out his fingers to count off the landmarks he'd seen.

"Houses of Parliament, Big Ben, Olympic Park, Tower Bridge..."

He was still listing places, but one had caught in Debra's mind.

"You were on Tower Bridge the day of the incident?" Debra interrupted.

Bloch looked at her blankly, but he nodded.

"I expect there were a lot of tourists there that day," Debra continued thoughtfully.

"Yes," Bloch said. Debra played out the silence, as she had with so many clients before. "Well," the murderer continued after a moment, "a lot of them stand on the bridge for pictures. I took a selfie, a really good one. I was there for a while, because other people asked me to take pictures for them."

A flush of terrified excitement rushed through Debra's chest. She fumbled with her notebook, sliding out the photograph. "Did you by any chance take this one?" she suggested.

She slid the photo across the table. Bloch looked down, and at first his face was as gaunt and blank as it had ever been. He was looking at two blurred faces after all. Debra watched his curious gaze travel over the figures in the picture, perhaps taking in those colorful nerdy t-shirts of theirs. Then, something broke. Bloch put a hand to his mouth with horror and a wild sob came from deep within his throat.

"Oh God, this is them," he whispered. "I'd have sworn I never met them before, but...I think I took this picture. A Japanese girl. She didn't have much English. There was a boyfriend who spoke even less. They had an instamatic camera, very old looking thing. No...please tell me this isn't them."

Bloch's cracked voice gave way to full-blown sobbing, and he threw his head against the table with a violent bang. Debra jumped at the impact and the sergeant rushed forward to restrain the killer. She snatched the photo away and hid it back in her bag. She got up from the table abruptly, her insides shaking at the echoing sound of Bloch's sobbing.

"I didn't mean to!" Bloch screamed. "Something made me do it!"

His temper was rising, fuelled by fear and grief. Debra watched him for one forlorn moment, gazing into his sorrowful eyes. She believed him. She believed that he had been overtaken by a force beyond his control.

"No more questions, thank you," she said.

When she managed to escape the interview room, she found Reggie heading down the corridor towards her. He was accompanied by a young man with perfectly coiffured hair, who looked up at Reggie as though he'd just found a new pop star to crush on. The young officer held a few files in his hands, almost absent-mindedly.

"Ah, Doctor Jasper," Reggie said in his best official tone. "This young man catalogued the scene of the crime, if you have any further questions."

She would never admit it, but Reggie Lexington really was a superb actor. He had the young officer in the palm of his hand, delivered to Debra like information on a silver platter. She thought carefully about what Bloch had just revealed.

"Was there a camera?" she asked the young man. "Did you recover an instamatic camera from the scene of the crime?"

The young officer thought for a moment, his pale lips pouting. Then, he shook his head. "No, if it was something fancy like that I'd have remembered," he replied. "We recovered a man-bag that must have belonged to Makoto, which had a digital camera in it."

Debra shook her head. "They had an instamatic too, I'm sure of it."

The officer opened one of his files and perused it thoughtfully. "It doesn't look like a camera was found at their hotel room either," he observed. "But... well, that's strange."

"What is?" Reggie coaxed, snooping at the file over the lad's shoulder.

"Well, there's no record of Sakiko's purse or passport," the officer revealed. "She didn't have a handbag with her at the theatre, but she didn't leave it at the hotel either. Something's gone missing somewhere."

The camera would be with the missing items, Debra was sure of it. But Bloch was caught at the scene of the crime moments later, and he hadn't stolen anything. He had no reason to, he wasn't even aware he'd done the killing at the time. The poor Swede was still screaming beyond the interview room door, and Debra felt the sting of tears in her eyes.

"Thank you for your help," she told the young officer, making to walk away.

"Oh, please take these for your investigation," the officer offered.

He handed her the files. How Reggie had managed to convince him to do that was beyond all reasoning.

"I asked young James here to rustle up a copy of the record so far, and he found a few similar cases in the recent past," Reggie explained. "I thought they might help you build Bloch's profile."

It almost looked like Reggie wanted to wink at her. He was proud of himself, so completely full of his own marvelous skills. Debra only gave him a nod, his bravado quelling some of her fears. She thanked James again for his efforts, and stuffed the confidential files into her bag so that no-one would question them on their way out of the station.

****

For all his skill with words, Reggie was lazy when it came to reading. The reports were thick and convoluted in their construction, and that meant it was time for the great actor to make an excuse and go home. That left Debra sitting at her breakfast bar late at night, perusing the file about the case. So far, she had come up with nothing unusual, save for the missing possessions that James had already spotted. She'd read the file several times, and it was with a sigh that she closed it and rubbed her tired eyes.

Perhaps the similar cases were worth a look. They were dated several months back from this particular incident, but Debra reasoned that unexplained and unmotivated murders had to be few and far between. The first of the unexplained cases was from Billericay in Essex, and it detailed the gruesome reality of a young man who had murdered his mother, grandfather and both his small children, but left his wife alive. His name was Archie Green, and he'd been sentenced to life imprisonment despite pleading innocence.

There were some interview transcripts in the file, and as Debra began to peruse them, she realized Archie pleaded a very similar case to Bloch:

I know I did it. I can remember doing it now. But I still don't know why. I don't remember anything leading up to the point where I picked up the knives. Something made me do it. Something made me snap.

Bloch had said exactly that: "Something made me do it." Debra read on through Archie's transcripts, learning that he was 'Arch' to his family, and his wife was Ally. He referred to her often, desperate to see her and explain once again that he never meant to destroy their family. Whenever his dead children were mentioned, Arch burst into uncontrollable tears and the interview had to be terminated. Even from the simple words on the page, Debra's analysis told her that this was a man who had not wanted to kill his family. Just as Anders Bloch didn't want to murder two people he'd only ever met once.

There was a final interview, just before Arch appeared in court, and the transcript appeared to show the ravings of a madman. Indeed, a psychologist had already signed off the page as evidencing insanity. Debra read this final page with interest, the hairs on her arms standing on end with every word:

I've figured it out. It's the camera. I took a photo of them all. The camera left Ally out. And I left Ally out. Don't you see? Everyone in the picture died! The camera killed them, not me! The camera! Find the camera!

Debra felt a wrench of sickness hit her stomach. She had felt drawn to the photograph of the dead victims and of the snapshot taken of what was left of the photo referenced by Archie. She suddenly wondered if it's strange distortion had not been caused by some unknown substance in her bag. What if the faces had faded after the deaths had happened, as if the photograph knew that its subjects were no longer alive? Anders Bloch had had no reason at all to hunt down and kill two random tourists. He didn't even have a ticket for the theatre that night. If the camera had driven him to do it...

The phone rang, and Debra jumped. As she fumbled for her mobile, she shook her head out of the sheer midnight madness which had enveloped her. The ideas she was having sounded like something from a horror story, and that was nothing to do with the science she had so furtively buried herself in for years and years of training. She answered the phone, grinning at her own foolishness.

"Hello?"

"Deb..."

It took her a moment to make out her own name amid the sobbing. The man who was crying on the phone had a slow, smooth tone usually, and it was hard to imagine him so broken and terrified.

"Reggie? Is that you?" Debra asked.

"I've done something terrible, Debra," Reggie sobbed. "I've killed Lyle."

****

It was three in the morning when Debra approached the Theatre Royal. Reggie waited by the stage door, pale as a ghost and dressed in a robe. As she entered the building, he explained he had discarded his clothes after they were covered in blood, and Lyle's body and the clothes were wrapped up in an old curtain backstage. Debra watched her long-time client carefully, studying the way he wrung his hands and ran his fingers frantically through his hair. He was a bitchy, jealous actor at times, but he was no killer. She could never believe that of him.

"Why did you do it?" Debra asked.

"I don't know," Reggie admitted. "I don't feel like I did. I saw my hands with the knife. I saw what they did, but they weren't my own. I was out of my body, Deb. I was totally..."

Tears fell from his eyes, darkened by his terror and the dim light of the theatre. Debra walked him back to his dressing room, and they sat among his lavish possessions as he cried out all his grief.

"He wasn't a bad actor," Reggie wailed. "He was quite good actually. And not bad looking, in the right light. He had a future. He had a future and I've gone and...oh God..."

Debra patted his shoulder, her mind wandering over the too-familiar scene of a sobbing murderer's confession. It was then that her gaze locked on a peculiar sight on Reggie's dressing table.

"Reg, why is there a ladies' handbag in here?" she asked.

"Oh," he sobbed, trying to clear his throat. "I was going to call you in the morning about it. I found that Japanese woman's bag. It's definitely hers, I checked the passport. It was in the theatre lost and found, reportedly left in the bathroom before the show started."

Debra reached out with a tentative hand, lifting the leather flap of the bag. Propelled by gravity, a vintage camera toppled out onto the table. It was silver in hue, but sleek and unusually compact for its kind. There was an adjustable lens at the front and a flash, as well as the slot where the instant pictures came out. Debra's fingertips lingered an inch away from the camera, tingling as though the very touch of it might burn her. Reggie wept quietly beside her.

"Did you *use* this, Reggie?" Debra said. "Did you use Sakiko's camera?"

He looked up, his face filled with regret. "I know it's a bit in poor taste, using a dead woman's things, but..." He took in a breath. "When I got back here, Lyle was celebrating his first night on stage. I felt sorry for the poor chap and he was having a party. There was booze. I thought, what harm could it do to show him some support for a change?"

"And you took a picture of him?" Debra asked.

Reggie nodded. "I took one of him first, then he took some of me and the girls. We only did a few shots before the film ran out."

Bloch's words hovered in Debra's head along with those of Archie Green. She could no longer deny the coincidence between the photographs and the murders. The device which sat innocently between her and Reggie had everything to do with the violent crimes that had been committed. Debra's heart quivered with the realization and her breath caught in her throat for a long moment.

"You said Lyle took some pictures of you and the chorus girls?" Debra checked.

"Yes," Reggie sniffed. "Why do you ask?"

Debra took a deep breath, steeling herself for the truth. "Because I think we need to go and be sure that he's definitely dead," she explained. "Your life could be in danger if he isn't."

It took a hell of a lot of persuading to get Reggie to revisit the scene of his crime. The backstage area of the Theatre Royal was a massive expanse, with a high cavernous ceiling that echoed every footfall. Shadows shifted amid the black curtains, and there was a veritable obstacle course of discarded props, stage lights, and speakers strewn about. Debra felt the blood before she saw it; the trail of curtain beneath her feet became sodden and damp. She and Reggie walked by the torchlight of her phone, the slim white beam trained on the bric-a-brac ahead.

"Where did you put him?" Debra pressed.

It was clearly painful for Reggie to relive the moment, but Debra had to know the details. The obstacles ahead were confusing enough without tripping over a corpse to boot.

"I wrapped him in one of the spare curtains on the floor," Reggie stammered. "Here, these are my clothes."

Beside a large stage light, one of Reggie's best designer shirts was soaked in crimson. Reggie paused, looking mournfully at his outfit, and then he looked around thoughtfully. His handsome brow furrowed into a worried knot of wrinkles above the bridge of his nose. He looked around again, and Debra began to feel uneasy.

"He's not here," Reggie said. "Lyle isn't here."

"That can't be right," Debra insisted.

She pushed past Reggie and began to search through the curtains, circulating the area around Reggie's stained clothes. She looked behind boxes and furniture, her torch beam leaving no spot unsearched. Sure enough, Reggie was right.

"So you didn't kill Lyle," she surmised.

"I did," Reggie interjected at once. His voice had taken on a low, dark tone. "I know what I did, Deb, even if it wasn't me doing it. I felt the knife plunge in. I cried over the poor bastard's body when I was covering him up. He was gone. There was no chance of-"

"Then how?" Debra demanded. "What are you suggesting, Reg? That Lyle's dead body got up and-"

Footsteps echoed somewhere nearby. The noise threw Reggie and Debra into silence, and they stared at each other in the half-light. Debra gulped and felt her mind mull over possibilities. If she was willing to believe in some sort of possession affecting those who handled the camera, then perhaps the idea of a dead man walking wasn't such a far cry from home. The prospect made her feel as though her spine was made of water, and every step she took became uneasy. She tiptoed back to Reggie, who reached out and enveloped her with one of his shaking arms.

"You don't think?" he whispered.

"No," Debra replied. "Impossible."

And yet, she feared the footsteps. In the echoing expanse, it was difficult to know which direction they were coming from, and Debra was loathe to turn off the light on her phone, even though she knew it would attract the attention of the stranger when they reached the stage. It was best to move away, to sneak back down the dark corridor and cloister themselves in the dressing room where they could safely call for help. Debra began to guide Reggie through the labyrinth of props, feeling suddenly queasy at the sodden squelch of blood beneath her feet.

Their agonizing pace made the fear double in Debra's nerves, waves of wild electricity hitting her fragile form. If she had previously been complaining about her boring, lonely life, she realized now she'd give anything to be at home in front of the TV. Reggie clung to her, gripping her waist with a strong hand, his tense fingers digging into her flesh a little. He was a killer. He had told her as much. Yet with him, she had always felt secure. She reached out in the dark, trying to find his other hand to hold it tightly.

But as she shifted, the torch beam caught a flash of something moving ahead.

Reggie was the first to shout out in panic, but when he did two high-pitched screams answered him. Debra threw the torch beam up into the corridor, illuminating two pale faces that squinted back with confusion. Debra recognized them at once, though she had never learned their names in all the time she'd been coming to the theatre for Reggie's appointments. He only ever referred to them as Blonde Patricia and Red Patricia. It was a reasonable certainty that Patricia wasn't either of their names. Debra merely gave them a nod, and tried to put a smile on her face. Nerves stretched her lips too thin, her teeth bared too much.

"It's all right girls, it's only us," she soothed. "What are you doing back here?"

Blonde Patricia had one hand over her heart, panting a little from the shock.

"We carried the party on at Spearmint Rhino for a while," she said in a high pitched voice, "and when Reggie texted to say we'd started up again, we hopped on the tube to come back over."

"Why are we all in the dark?" Red Patricia added. "We tried to do the lights when we got in, but the switches aren't working."

Debra felt Reggie squeeze her where he held her close. The Patricia's watched him with interest. Debra supposed it must have looked very unusual to see Reggie Lexington clinging to a woman.

"First of all, I do not text," Reggie clarified. "Far too gauche. And I couldn't have texted you if I'd wanted to. My phone's back in the dressing room."

Debra gulped, pushing at a lump in her throat that simply wouldn't go down. "Then there's someone else here," she breathed. "Come on, back to the exit. We need to go, now!"

She and Reggie hurried the Patricia's up the corridor, their confused protests hanging in the air. The girls assured them that they had entered via the stage door only minutes ago, but when the foursome arrived at the exit where the little box and the visitor's book sat, they found the door closed and locked…from the outside. Reggie made the ladies stand aside, putting his back into every shove and shake of the handle. They were well and truly locked in, and the door was made of old Georgian wood, thick and impenetrable.

"This is one of those times when I wish we worked in a ghastly modern theatre," Reggie said, panicked. "There'd be glass walls that you could smash, and all the doors would be made of balsa wood or some other eco-friendly shit."

"We're trapped," Blonde Patricia sobbed, clinging to her friend.

"But why?" Red Patricia added in an angrier tone. "Whose sick joke is this?"

Debra and Reggie exchanged a look, silent agreement passing between them. Nobody could know what Reggie had done. They wouldn't understand if they did, they couldn't know the wicked and terrible influence of the camera.

"We think it's Lyle," Debra told the girls. "If you see him, don't linger. He's...drunk. He's drunk out of his mind and it's bloody terrifying."

"Lyle?" Red Patricia asked, one copper brow raised. "He's a puppy. He damn-near wet himself before he went on tonight. You're trying to tell me that Lyle could be-"

A low, mournful cry interrupted the girl's words. Incensed by fear, the foursome began to scatter, and Debra tried to whisper to them all to regroup.

"No, don't! We must stay together!"

But her insistence was to no avail. Only Reggie listened, returning to her side and holding her shoulders as they stood stock still. The Patricia's had vanished from the torchlight, and when Debra shone the beam around, she only saw their heels as they pelted down the corridor which led out to the main auditorium. She looked at Reggie, and he cast one more glance to the locked door beside them.

"Perhaps we could hide in the guard's box?" he suggested, observing the little off-shoot with the window that Stan usually sat at.

"We have to go get the girls," Debra urged. "I don't want to. Believe me, I want to hide, but they'll die. If Lyle is up and about, then the camera's got him under its possession. He won't have control. He'll be just like you were, Reg."

Reggie gulped, and gave a single, solemn nod. "Onward then," he murmured.

The public area of the Theatre Royal was just as large as the backstage space, with numerous bars, bathrooms and waiting areas for the couple of thousand people who frequented the place to gather. When Debra and Reggie passed through the doorway that led from one to the other, they found the tall windows of the building's glorious frontage let in plenty of moonlight. Debra turned off her torch, her phone slick in her sweat-soaked hand.

"We should call the police," she mused.

"But then they'll know," Reggie said with a pleading note. "If we call them in now, they'll find my clothes. Even if Lyle's not dead, they'll take me away."

He reached out, holding Debra's hands. The phone was between their palms, but he didn't try to take it. His grey eyes shone in the light of the moon, damp with fear and sorrow. Debra sighed, and put the phone back in her pocket. So long as they could find a way out, the police could wait. All they had to do was find the Patricia's, and get to one of the emergency exits that the public used. Those doors would surely open easier than those backstage.

"Pity the windows are original," Debra mused, observing the wrought iron grid between each of the small glass panels.

There was a scream from somewhere ahead. Debra picked up the pace, following as fast as her trembling feet would allow, racing through the foyer and the downstairs bar. The echoing sound could only be coming from inside the massive auditorium itself, the grisly scene where the Japanese couple had met their fate only a day earlier. To Debra's surprise, Reggie was the first to reach the double doors that would lead them in. He smashed them open with a push of his broad shoulders and they clattered with an echoing bang. The sound shot through the space, and a woman looked up from some fifteen feet away where she stood among the seats. It was Blonde Patricia, and she looked like she'd seen a ghost.

"We only got separated for a moment," she said, her whole body trembling.

She was looking down into the seats, sobs wracking her chest, and Debra could already imagine exactly what lay on the floor between them.

"It's Red, isn't it?" Reggie asked across the echoing expanse. Blonde Patricia nodded. "Did he stab her?"

"No," the blonde chorus girl replied. "She's been strangled with something."

That didn't fit the pattern. Debra felt a new wave of fear shake through her, and before she even had time to fully react, a shadow leapt up from the rows of seats. He moved like a shark towards Blonde Patricia, and no amount of shouting from either Debra or Reggie could make her move in time. They watched, aghast, as a black-clad figure took a length of wire and swiftly wrapped it around the girl's neck. She was garrotted in seconds, slumping to the floor with a horrific choking sound.

There was no time to grieve. There was only time to run.

Debra and Reggie streaked hand in hand through the theatre, racing towards the nearest emergency exit. When they reached the modern grey door made of sheet metal, Reggie threw his whole body at the release bar. As the cold air of a London night hit them both squarely in the face, they began to cry with relief. Reggie had tumbled to the ground from his feat of strength, and Debra fumbled to pick him up so that they could make the rest of their escape. As she did so, however, another sound made them jump.

"Hey! You two!"

The voice sounded oddly familiar, but in her panic Debra couldn't place it. They both looked back to the emergency exit, into the blackness of the theatre building.

And somebody took their picture.

****

"It can't have been that camera," Debra insisted. "You told me you used up the shots."

Reggie paused at his nail biting for a moment. "There was another pack of film in Sakiko's bag," he revealed.

"Jesus, why didn't you tell me that before?" Debra raged.

"I..." Reggie stumbled. "I didn't know then that the camera was responsible. You just said we had to check Lyle's body. We should have kept it with us."

Neither of them had seen who took the photograph. It was seven in the morning of that same awful day, and London was beautiful from the window of Debra's apartment. It a city waking, ready for its exciting new day, but she and Reggie were fraught with terror. It was only a matter of hours between the photos being taken and the victims being killed, and that all depended on how fast the killer found its victims.

"Grab all the toiletries and throw them in here," Debra urged, handing Reggie a wash bag.

"Right," he said, his voice trembling. "Good. I need something to do with my hands. Christ, I'm such a wreck."

"Actually, I'm sort of impressed," Debra said with a forlorn sort of sigh. "In our sessions, you always make yourself out to be so hapless, like you can't do anything without support. But here you are, breaking down doors and keeping me safe."

"We kept each other safe," Reggie reasoned. He hung his head for a moment, then took in a breath. "To be honest, I only say those things so you'll keep coming to see me. I like your company, Deb. You're the only decent friend I've got."

It was strange to see the actor not acting. Some of that lonely little hole in Debra's heart flooded with his words. She couldn't believe it had taken something like this to make them real friends, and in a strange way, she was glad for it. If they could survive, they could be proper companions, who'd shared their darkest fears and secrets. If they had a future, then it could be a bright one. Debra leaned over and kissed Reggie's cheek, and he gave her a broken little smile.

"We'd better go, the train leaves at seven-thirty," she said.

The journey to the station was horrific. Everywhere she looked Debra saw people who could be the potential killer. She had no idea whose face could be that of her soon to be murderer. She reasoned that she and Reggie were just like Makoto and Sakiko now, except that the young couple had at least been blissfully oblivious to the stranger who was coming to cut their heads off with a set of blades. Debra's eyes were everywhere at the station, every person with their hands in a bag or their pockets, waiting for the silver knives to emerge and glint in the morning sunlight.

Even when they got on the train, their luggage on their knees amid the overcrowded carriage, Debra's mind was ablaze with fear. Reggie bought tea from the woman with the trolley, but Debra was shaking too much to hold her cup.

"You've got to have something, dear girl," he urged.

"Is this how it's going to be?" Debra asked, in a voice so hollow it sounded like she'd abandoned it. "Always looking over our shoulders? Never being able to stay in one place?"

Reggie leaned close to her ear, inspecting the other passengers warily.

"It's better than being dead, isn't it?" he observed.

And of course it was. His hands were pale, clasping the cups with tense fingers. Debra couldn't imagine how much worse it was for Reggie, for not only had he escaped the clutches of their mystery photographer for now, but he still had the savage memory of Lyle's murder to process. He was damaged, perhaps beyond repair, and Debra was his only source of healing. She would have to do her best for him now.

"Check your phone for the news," Reggie suggested. "The guard will have opened up for the morning check by now. The bodies will be all over the media, I'm sure of it. Those poor girls...and poor Lyle..."

Debra did as she was told. Her phone was nearly dead from the night before, but she managed to load a search and type in the theatre's name. She scrolled for a moment, her brow furrowed.

"There's nothing," she announced.

"What?" Reggie said in amazement.

"I mean, there's new reports on the Japanese couple's killing, but there's nothing new," she explained. "No new discoveries. Nothing at all."

"But how?" Reggie demanded. "I mean, why not?"

He began to ramble on the topic, supposing the different ways in which the news had been concealed. Perhaps the guard was late, or in so much shock that he had not yet telephoned the police. Or perhaps Lyle, if indeed it was Lyle who had killed the girls, was keeping the Royal under lock and key. If the camera could raise the dead, then who knew what other powers it possessed. Debra heard all of these thoughts in the background, but none of them sunk in. The whole night had been a mess and part of her knew she was going into shock still over it all. Who knew what happened at that theatre after they left.

"One thing, though," Reggie said, pulling her from her wondering. His eyes were green by the morning light, swimming with fear. "What happened to the instamatic camera?"

Debra didn't know and didn't want to know. That thing was going to haunt them the rest of their lives. She never wanted to think about it again.

****

In the dark confines of the theatre, Stan the guard had finished cleaning up the blood. He'd killed those two dopey showgirls – the bitches who'd made fun of him every night when they passed his window – in the very same spot where the police had finished their investigation into the other strange homicides. Stan had been watching the case with interest, and when Doctor Jasper had begun to speak of the camera, Stan was listening. There were security cameras in every room and corridor of that theatre, including the dressing room of that great fop Reggie Lexington.

Stan even had footage of Lexington stabbing Lyle Waite to death. He had watched it several times over already, fascinated by the frantic monster that Lexington had become. He had watched that actor turn rabid and thrust the knife again and again into the understudy's body. If Doctor Jasper was to be believed, then the little silver camera was the cause for such a wild spree of mayhem. That same camera sat on Stan's desk, beside his shiny digital one, inside the little office where he kept the visitor's book.

It would make his job so much more interesting from now on. When the new cast came in to replace those who had vanished, there would surely be more upper class actors looking down their noses at the humble guard, and more girls ready to tease him. But now, Stan would have the ideal solution. A new pack of film had been loaded into the instamatic. Stan would simply invite anyone he didn't like to take a photo of someone else he didn't like. One would die horribly, and the other would suffer for life in prison.

The Camera Monstura, as Stan liked to call it, was the ideal tool to keep him company on those long, lonely stints at the stage door office. He wouldn't need to watch TV on his phone any more.

Murder was a far more entertaining sport.

Cacophony

Cooper adjusted the telescope's eyepiece. Huddled over, a bare silhouette against the starry sky, Ed thought he looked like a hobo trying to start a fire in his 44 gallon drum. "What are we doing out here Coop?" He took a swig from the hip-flask he had been absently tapping a moment before, and then adjusted his seat. "I would've been more comfortable at your place y'know." Only the wind gave a response, gently coercing the surrounding tree branches into twitching. The leaves shook and conspired as if alive, whispering to each other in the night. Ed took another drink and reached over for the flashlight with his spare hand. He switched it on and let the beam wander.

They were situated on a bare patch of earth, maybe twenty feet across. Tufts of grass and several trees crowded around the clearing, encircled themselves by denser patches of woodland interspersed with rocky outcroppings. After that, the rough plateau – a mile or so across – dropped off into steeper inclines, sometimes sheer cliffs. A single path, a fire-trail, provided access to the summit; from there, only a handful of trees obstructed views of endless vaults of black sky. Ed's car was parked alongside the closest actual road, a half an hour walk away.

"*Cooper!*" His voice, having nothing to echo against, raced off into the night and didn't turn back.

Coop looked up from the eyepiece. "Yes?"

"What are we doing out here again man?" The torch beam meandered around the dirt at their feet. "I would've liked to hang out at your place."

"We're looking for Pla—hey, can you switch that thing off?" Darkness fell across the ground after his harsh request. "Thanks. We're looking for Planet Nine." Cooper was again a shadow against the horizon.

"And we couldn't have just got drunk in your backyard?" Ed sounded like a sulking teen.

"You sound drunk already. Pass that here." The black shape moved closer, and then a moment of awkwardness before Coop relieved the hip-flask from his friend's hand. He took a sip and laughed. "It's finished already? We probably can't drive back 'til morning now." Cooper didn't have his driver's license. He laughed again, tossed the flask in the rough direction of their backpacks, and walked back to his original position. "No...no, Ed, we couldn't have just gotten wasted on the deck-chairs." His friend grumbled something and began ruffling through their bags. "There's too much artificial light at my place. Look around...nothing here but us and the night sky."

"Can I switch the torch on again?" Sulking teen.

"Yeah, go for it."

The beam of light confined itself to the interior of one of the backpacks. Cooper looked over and saw his friend smile in the dimness before the flashlight switched off again. Ed sat back down.

"You want another sip man?" The sound of swallowing could be heard clearly over the breeze. "Ah, that's good." He leaned back in his fold-able chair. It made a slipping sound against the rocky dirt. "Shit dude, is this chair made for kids?" He heard laughter in the darkness and joined in. Thirty seconds of adjustment went by before Ed was finally leaning back comfortably. He took a victory swig. "OK, OK...tell me about Planet Nine."

"Well, I told you on the phone, remember? I gave you every chance to come Ne-"

"Yeah, yeah, I know. But it's been two months since we've caught up bro."

"Fair enough." Cooper paused for a second, licking his lips. "They only discovered it in January, so it doesn't have a proper name yet, just Planet Nine, but they're thinking of calling it 'Bowie', apparently." He chuckled.

"What? Are you serious?" The trees rustled in the ebb of the wind.

"Yeah, they discovered it a couple of weeks after he died."

Ed took a sip and listened to the leaves. "That's kinda cool."

"You kidding? It's awesome!" Cooper's smile failed to light up the dark. It was his turn to sound like a kid. "And tonight, there's actually a chance we can spot it."

"You mean no one's seen it yet?"

"Nope, they only detected it indirectly. But tonight they say it should be visible."

Ed took a sip. "Cool." He followed it with a longer drink and a belch. "So is that the 'scope we looked at the moon through on New Years?"

"Yeah, the Konasky. It's a Newtonian Refle..." -ctor Telescope; Coop finished the sentence mentally. "Uh, it's a good 'scope." He let out a short laugh. "If Nine does come into view, the Konasky should be able to show us a good amount of detail. But the most *interesting* part..." His voice took on a measure of awe, "... is that all these astronomers have different ideas about its position in the sky. They think some kind of unique conjunction will occur tonight."

"Like, planets aligning kinda deal?" He burped again, quieter this time.

"Yeah, exactly." Cooper's shadow shuffled over and Ed held out the flask; a wandering hand quickly retrieved it. "I mean, it's already counter-aligned with six other objects, which is how they-"

"Uh?"

"It's OK, it's not important." The wind picked up, almost reaching a low howl before dying back down again just as suddenly. "Basically, there's all these different ideas about what the significance of its position in the sky."

"So you gonna take a drink or what?"

"Yeah, yeah." Sounds of swallowing. "Calm your farm, here you go."

"Where?" Hands reached out in the darkness. "Ah." Ed smiled and took another sip once he'd found the flask. "You know astrology is bullshit, right?"

"The stuff in the papers, of course it is. Hey, can I have one more?" The drink-passing ritual took place again; it was a little more seamless this time. Ed didn't feel fully comfortable until the flask took up residence in his hand again.

"So what is there besides the newspaper stuff?"

"Well, I don't know. Just, the idea in general I guess." Cooper's voice grew more serious. He was still standing near the chair and his black specter loomed large as it gestured against the night sky. "It's an old idea, alchemists, occultists. They were all in on it. The microcosm and macrocosm."

"The micro..." Ed laughed. "We should've taken joints up here instead of whiskey bro."

"Yeah, probably." Coop laughed too.

"OK, tell me about what the cultists were up to then, I'm listenin'."

"*Occultists.*"

"Yeah, them too." Ed smiled.

"Well, they just saw correlations. What goes on up there somehow ties into down here. And we all bang our heads against the wall trying to figure it out." Coop's gesturing had stopped, but his shadow remained close by. There were no clouds in sight, just the dizzying array of stars.

"I guess that kinda makes sense..."

"Think about it." Cooper's shadow swayed into a shuffling semi-pace while he talked. "Couldn't the solar system – the whole *universe* – be a giant, interconnected organism? One that we can never fully understand?"

"Hmmm." Ed followed his friend's shape as it moved to and fro.

"Or think about it like a machine. Imagine that all of reality is one huge machine, and we can only see the workings of a few of the gears." Coop paused, picturing what he was saying in his mind. "Every now and then a huge pendulum or some other bit of machinery swings into view, and we don't know what to make of it. *But*, we can see that its movement correlates to the few gears we *do* know about. And so we're left wondering at the pendulum's significance..." He trailed off.

"Yeah, that makes more sense."

Cooper's voice lowered. "Maybe our ancestors knew something we didn't." He stopped pacing and moved back toward the telescope. Ed leaned forward in his chair.

"Something to do with the stars?"

"Yes." Cooper trod on an unseen rock as he maneuvered around the 'scope; he almost lost balance before kicking the offender off into the night. "I mean, almost every ancient civilization knew the night sky and its movements incredibly well. *Really* well, you know?" He didn't wait for an answer. "Not only could they navigate by it and tell the exact date, they projected their entire mythology onto it. The stories that have been told, for each and every one of these stars."

The young men looked up into the cloudless sky. The air was still, and the leaves strangely hushed. Ed was first to break the silence.

"But...not Planet Nine." He paused, unsure of himself. "Right?"

"*Exactly.*"

Ed thought Cooper sounded like one of those deranged scientists from a 50s sci-fi film. He suppressed a giggle by busying his mouth with whiskey before waiting for his friend to go on. But there was silence. It had an expectancy to it, and Ed felt it was his job to continue. "So...there's no-one left to put this planet in a... into a mythology?"

"More or less." Coop was busy with the telescope, but his voice was still clear. "I mean, scientists will classify it, but not many shamans will, y'know."

Ed stopped the flask before it reached his mouth. "Ohhh, I dunno, aren't there a ton of druids and all that in the UK?" He completed the swig.

"Kind of, but, it's not the same." Cooper walked back over to his friend. "Can you pass the flashlight again?"

"Yeah man." Ed fumbled flash and flask. "Here."

"Thanks." Coop switched the light on and grabbed a rectangular plastic box that sat on top of his backpack. He opened it, took out a small circular object, then closed the lid and replaced the box. He gave Ed back the light and resumed life as a silhouette.

Ed put the flashlight on his lap, then leaned back into semi-comfort. "Lens?"

"Yeah, it's just a different lens. Well, filter." The Cooper-figure huddled over the telescope.

"Wait, d'you need it again? The light?" Silence. "Coop?"

"Nah, I'm all good. Umm, where were we?"

"Shamans." Ed had a sudden flash of Cooper as a shaman, intent on completing some unknown ritual, telescope for a May-pole. He grinned into the night and rewarded himself with a drink.

"Right. So, back then you had shamans giving knowledge to the people, now you have scientists. Each one is responsible for delivering a different kind of information. You follow?"

"Yeah, I follow."

"So, for the past however long we've been saying scientists are the shit."

"And?"

"And what if they're not?"

The trees resumed their whispering song. Both men lapsed into silence and stargazing; Coop with aid of his telescope, Ed with aid of his whiskey. The wide belt of the Milky Way crossed the sky above their heads, ending like a nocturnal rainbow at the thin crescent of the moon. Ed's voice sounded thin too, barely making the journey to his friend's ears. "Do you think tha-"

"Huh?"

Ed coughed a couple of times before speaking up. "Do you think the shamans could see? You reckon they could see gears we can't?" To Ed, machinery was more comfortable than mysticism.

"Yeah, I think so. I think we've been training ourselves for a long time to not see certain sets of gears." Cooper's voice got gradually quieter as he diverted attention to the telescope. From very far off, the cry of what sounded like a night-bird arrived on the soft wind. "Holy shit, I think I've got it..." Coop's voice was animated. "Yep, I think so!"

"Planet Nine?"

"Yeah, 'Bowie'. Hold on, I need the light." His shadowed form was swift in the inky black, and Ed almost fell off the chair when Coop bumped into him. "Sorry." The flashlight changed hands and a different circular object was retrieved from the plastic box. The light stayed on while Cooper fumbled with the filter replacement. "I can give you a look in a sec, I'll just make sure we can see details."

"Did you want another drink man?" After twenty seconds of no response, Ed took a swig.

"OK." Cooper switched off the flashlight and put it down next to the bags. He walked back over to the telescope. A minute passed. Ed wondered if the plateau was always this quiet. He took another swig, spilling a trickle of whiskey down his chin. Coop's voice was quiet again. "Hm."

"What is it man?" He wiped the whiskey off with his free hand. "Look cool?"

"It looks...fucking...I don't know. Can you do me a favor?"

"Wait, it looks what?" The wind began to pick up. "What are you seeing dude?"

"I don't know. It looks..."

"Dude, like *what*?"

"Like towers or something."

"What? Towers?" Ed finally mustered the initiative to get up off his chair. "I can't hear you man, it's too windy." He inched forward, swaying gently, trying not to knock over his friend, the telescope, or himself. The tree branches began shaking with more force, more intent, and the wind's distant howl struggled to be heard over the furious rustling of leaves. By gradual degrees, Ed made his way to Cooper's side without knocking anything over. The wind was keeping up but the howl died down. "I can't hear you man. Did you say there's towers?"

"*Yes*, I'm sure of it. Look." He moved to the side. "Give me your drink first. And don't bump the 'scope." The hip-flask exchanged hands.

"Yeah, yeah, chill out." Ed bent over the eyepiece, hands on knees, and struggled to keep his head steady.

Cooper leaned back and peered through the night, as if trying to see the planet with his naked eyes. He took a sip from the flask. "So can you see them?"

"I dunno dude, they look like mountains or something."

Coop looked back down. "They're definitely not mountains." He shuffled closer to his friend. "C'mon, stop hogging."

"What?" Ed stumbled back and started laughing. "That's the first time I've looked all night!" Cooper moved over to him and pressed the flask back into his friend's hand. "Look, can you do me a favor or what?" The whiskey was back at home.

"Yeah, yeah, gimme a sec." Ed slid his right foot out in front of him as a forward scout, and messily made his way back to the chair. "Yeah alright, what ya want." He upended the hip-flask, drained the last of the liquid, and tossed it toward the bags. "Hmm?"

"Do you have your phone on you?"

"Yeah."

"Can you go to the astronomy forums and see if anyone else is reporting this?"

"Yeah, but fuckin' astrologers dude, d'you really-"

"*Astronomers*, Edward."

"Oh." Ed stared blankly ahead into the darkness for a half a minute, before awkwardly sliding his mobile phone out of his back pocket. He fumbled for a handful of seconds, then found the right button. The screen's brightness caused him to wince and turn away. "*Fuck*, man." He turned back to the phone, squinting, and – after another minute – opened a search engine. "Alright, what do I type?" Cooper was hunched over the telescope. The wind began to rally its distant howl once more. "*Oi!* What do I type man?"

"Sorry." He didn't look up from the eyepiece. "Try..." The leaves and howl competed for dominance. It wasn't clear whether Cooper finished the sentence or not.

"Yeah?" Ed found it annoying having to continually speak up. "Try what?"

"Just try 'Planet Nine visual observation' or something."

Ed started hitting the screen with his forefinger. "What about 'towers'?"

"Just try what I said first."

"OK, what was it again?"

Cooper sighed to himself and turned around; facing the black shape seated a few feet away. "Try typing Plane-"

"Ah shit."

"What?"

"I don't have signal."

Cooper paused for a moment. "What? We're in a good spot. There should be signal here somewhere. They just built those new towers I thought."

"Yeah, well guess we're not close enough to one of those rare towers." Ed turned the screen around and pointed it accusingly at his friend. Coop spun his head away from the phone.

"OK, I believe you. You'll fuck up my night vision."

A voice called out in the distance, making itself heard between two loud gusts of wind. Ed almost leaped out of his chair into a standing position. "What the fuck was that?" Silence. "Did you hear that?" Ed's whisper was fierce enough to be understood over the wind. "Did you fucking hear that?" He looked around frantically but felt surrounded by an endless company of lumbering dark shapes. Nothing looked familiar. From the distance came the crack of splintering wood.

"I heard it, it sounded-"

Again, a voice. A stifled yell almost. Closer this time. Ed felt unsure of his limbs as he spun about in the darkness; they felt shaky, weak, useless. He bumped into Cooper. "Um, is there…uh, dude, can we-"

"Ed, calm down, be quiet." Coop could hear an unfamiliar terror in his friend's voice, a terror which inspired a seemingly unending stream of incoherent babble. "Dude, it's OK, just keep quiet for me." He reached out and put a hand on his friend's shoulder. Ed calmed down somewhat. A second later, they both became aware of a faint rumbling sound.

Ed returned to panic. "The light, the *light*…where's the *fucking light!?*"

"What? Don't you have it?" From far off, another yell issued from a slightly different direction. Then more splintering wood.

"No! You used it to get…" He trailed off and fell to his knees, scrambling, searching. The rumbling grew closer. "I gave it to you man, *I gave it to you.*"

The memory of putting the flashlight on the ground leaped back into Cooper's head. Before he could join his friend in the search, the shadows in the near distance began to move. It was hard to tell how far away it was, but the rumbling was coming from there. "Get up." His friend scrabbled amongst the backpacks. "Ed, get up, now." Coop grabbed his arm and hoisted Ed to his feet. Although he probably couldn't see the gesture in the dark, Cooper spun his friend around and pointed. "Look, it's coming."

Ed didn't need to look twice, he immediately started running in the opposite direction. Four steps later he tripped and went sprawling face first over a patch of rocky ground. Hot pain assaulted his face, forcing a strangled cry from his lungs. Ed could feel dirt and pebbles mixing with blood in his mouth, in his eyes. He felt hands helping him up a few seconds later.

"Hold on."

Coop grabbed him and they immediately broke into an aimless, anxious escape. After stumbling through low-lying shrubs they broke out into a more open area. Directly ahead, the thin sickle of the moon looked down at them from low on the horizon, affording them a little more light. They increased their speed, but the rumbling was gaining steadily behind them and around them. Cooper's chest and throat burned with every desperate breath. His friend was faltering.

"C'mon Ed, c'mon..."

Their crazed and jumbled flight across the plateau wore on for sixty agonizing seconds, before the rumble resolved itself into an identifiable sound. It was running feet. Dozens and dozens of running feet. And they were almost upon them.

Cooper chanced a few fleeting backward glimpses, but it was hard to make anything out. The pursuers were silent now; any yelling had stopped. Somehow, that was even more terrifying – the isolated but mad flurry of a hundred or more intent feet, wordlessly closing in on their prey. As the rumble closed the final distance, Coop could hear breathing and panting underneath the muted stampede. It sounded like there could have been female voices as well. He went to risk another glance behind him, but was cut off: something blunt crashed into the back of his head and there was blackness.

****

Pain brought Cooper back to consciousness. He was still, but moving. It felt like he was floating upwards through an endless night. A fresh swell of pain made him wince. There was a stickiness at the back of his head, and a tightness pressing against the length of his body. He rocked unevenly from side to side. *I'm being carried.* It felt like he was in a giant hessian cocoon. Coop could tell now he was facing skyward, the blood pooling at the back of his head. It felt like a lot of blood. From the way he was swaying, it felt like there was one person at his feet and one person at his head, maneuvering him with what felt like relative ease. *Are they even people?*

The bumping, jostling ride slowed its pace. Mumbles could be heard, but it was hard to make out any articulation, let alone words. They stopped for a minute. The only sound Cooper could hear was the gentle creak of rope on wood, buttressed by an almost imperceptible rustling of leaves in the wind. A short, sharp sound issued from somewhere above his head and they began moving again. It felt like they were descending. *I mustn't have been out long if we're still getting down off the plateau.* He could hear rocks crunching underfoot. He went to reach a hand up to feel his head wound and realized his hands were bound. It wasn't overly tight, but it felt secure. Depressingly secure. Cooper changed tactic and worked his head against the sack he was being carried in. The weave was somewhat loose, and through it he could see several gray, seemingly cloaked shapes silhouetted against the night sky. All were silent. They gradually changed position until it looked like they arranged in a long single file.

The stars disappeared from view and Coop was aware of something only a few feet from him. He could detect a very faint flickering light – firelight, from up ahead maybe – that illuminated the surface which now replaced the sky. It looked like a cave wall. The feeling of descent continued. Cooper closed his eyes and wondered if Ed was still alive, being carried and cocooned in a similar rope-like prison. *Time to turn into a butterfly.* The pain began swelling almost unbearably. He made a small groan then bit his lip. *They can't know I've woken up.* He closed his eyes and tried to ride the waves of pain. But Coop slipped beneath the surface, back into unconsciousness.

****

"COOPER!"

Grunting sounds issued from all around. The stickiness still cloyed at the back of Coop's head. And it still hurt like all hell. He opened his eyes and saw a red-faced Ed to his left, tied to a rough-hewn metal rung that looked set in the cavern floor behind them. He turned around further and saw that his own hands were now bound behind his back, and a similar rope attached him to the same ancient-looking rung. Its metal was black, flecked with deep red. Cooper looked up and gradually back around until he faced forward again. The cloaked shapes surrounded them at a distance of twenty or so feet, huddled against the cave walls. There were at least a hundred figures moving in short, agitated bursts. A very small fire popped and crackled a few feet behind them, providing the only light. Overall, the cavern was roughly circular and fifty feet in diameter. There was a huge gaping void in front of them and off to the right. It appeared to slope downward, into the earth. Cooper turned further to the right and saw that a smaller passage led into the cave behind them. He spun back around and saw Ed was grinning at him. His face was streaked with blood.

"I thought you'd never wake up buddy." He sounded almost happy, and far more sober than when Cooper saw him last.

"Do you know how long I've been out?" Every word he spoke made the back of his head ring in agony. "Uh, my head's killing me."

"At least an hour." Ed looked around and nodded at the shifting crowd. "You got any idea who these masked fuckwits are?"

Cooper looked again and saw that the cloaked figures were indeed masked. He turned slowly. From where he sat he could see the devilish smiles carved into them, etched out in black, white, and red paint. The eye holes were slanted and the forehead had an image of something with tentacles on it. One turned to look directly at Cooper and he flinched at the sight. Red tears of blood splattered the front of the mask and made him suck in a breath.. "No man." He looked again at Ed. "No, I don't know."

"Well, what about that." Ed thrust his head forward and up this time. "You know what it's for?"

Coop followed his friend's gesture and saw that in the cavern's roof, directly ahead of them, there was a long shaft cut into the rock. The firelight was low enough that he could see a small rectangle of stars through the long aperture. "Judging by the angle, it's for us." He kept looking at the stars, spellbound. "Or we're here for it." The figures continued shuffling erratically. A crack issued from the fire behind them and the angle of light in the room changed slightly. The difference was enough to make the cavern walls take on a new countenance. From somewhere deep in the mountain, a huge, guttural sound reverberated with an almost physical force. Coop's mouth dropped open and he looked at Ed.

"Yep, that's the third time I've heard that. Don't know what the fuck it is though."

Cooper looked back at the aperture. Although the starlight couldn't have caused it, his face did seem to be aglow. "Hey. Yeah, I thought..." He squinted. "I know that star...no, not a star." His head turned slowly toward his friend. "I fucking know what this shaft is pointed at." He stared into Ed's eyes. "Bowie."

Ed grunted a laugh before spitting a large glob of bloody saliva to his left. "Are you for real?"

"Yes." Cooper started laughing himself. "Yes, I am. It's to welcome Planet Nine." The pain in his head didn't seem so bad anymore. The cadence of the grunting increased a notch. "It's for the new planet! It's for *Bowie!*"

"Yeah, OK dude, but I think we have more important thi-"

A thunderous, deep bellowing sound rent Ed's sentence in two. It came from the direction of Cooper's right foot. The noise of the cloaked mass raised itself in kind, both in volume and in pitch. Ed turned his shocked face slowly away from his friend and began to peer into the gloom at the figures around him. Cooper glanced at the huge black entryway off to his right, and then up and left to the aperture. He was grinning. "We don't have more important things Ed."

"Dude."

"We've been drawn to this specific place, at this specific time..."

"Coop."

"... called in to witness the daw-"

"*Oi!*" He didn't yell, but Ed put enough intensity into the word that it stopped Cooper's rant short. "Do you know what they're doing?"

"What? No, they're pro-"

"They're having sex, man."

Cooper looked around. Ed was right. "Well, I'd be fucking someone too in order to celebrate the alignment!" He grinned. "Even as the sacrifice, we-"

"So they are going to fucking sacrifice us?" Ed rolled his head toward the cavern's roof. "I *knew* it, knew these fu-"

"It's a *glory*, it's a *triumph!*" Cooper lowered his voice again. "For thousands of years we were ignorant of this thing, this planet, this Nine, and now it's being born and these people knew about it, they fucking *knew* about it and..."

"And what?"

"And built a *cathedral* for it." Cooper's face glowed in the gloom.

"This is a pretty shit cathedral if you ask me."

Both friends were silent and looked at each other for a few moments before laughing softly through bloody faces. Cooper stopped first. "I think it's a beautiful temple."

Ed shook his head and turned away. A roaring sound ripped out of the black entrance to their right, drowning out every other sound and increasing in volume before cutting off suddenly. Both their heads were left ringing in the afterglow.

Ed's face started to convulse in spasms of fear. "We're fucking done for man." He scrambled backward until the rough-hewn rung was between him and the cavernous gateway. "We're done, we're done."

Cooper stayed where he was, several feet closer to the roaring void than Ed. He smiled and looked away from it, turning his head again to the aperture. His face lit up. *"I can see it."*

"WE'RE DONE FOR YOU FUCKING IDIOT!" Ed shuffled forward on his knees to his friend, falling heavily onto Coop's shoulder. "IT'S HERE, IT'S HERE AND-"

"Look!" The naked passion in Cooper's voice broke the stream of yelling. Ed didn't actually look, but gibbered softly to himself incoherently, and focused on the huge black opening. He pressed closer into his friend's back. Coop didn't notice. "It's finally here." A high-pitched whirring sound sprang from the larger cave entrance, slicing through the din with the precision of a fine blade. Cooper's eyes remained fastened on the new planet. "We were chosen amongst them all Ed." The roar began again with grating ferocity from underneath the high-pitched drone. "Chosen to celebrate the birth-" His words grew gradually quieter, before being finally blown apart by a thunderous boom as if the earth itself were exploding into a thousand pieces. Gallons of fluid burst forth from the huge black entryway, concealing huge chunks of jelly-like material that sprayed across the chamber's opposing wall. It almost knocked Cooper off his knees, but his smiling face remained locked in an unknown magnetism, aligned with the cavern aperture.

A colossal, writhing nightmare burst forth from the bowels of the mountain, knocking a dozen cloaked figures over as it entered. Ed's scream was shrill, as if trying to match the pitch of the whirring drone. His mind would never again hold a sane thought.

Cooper didn't see the hulking leviathan, the horror from the pit; he saw only the planet. Bowie. He smiled. "I... I will be king."

Around him, the grunting, whirring, screaming, climaxing, and roaring combined into a feverish maelstrom, an extended heart attack. Ed's scream was the closest, repeating mechanically, over and over and over, drowning out his friend's voice. Coop began singing as loud as he could, his chest thrust forward. *"THOUGH NOTHING..."* Something resembling a gigantic, ropy tentacle smashed into the roof above with terrifying force. *"... WILL DRIVE THEM AWAY..."* Debris, rocks, and several small boulders tumbled down around them. Planet Nine was still in sight. *"OH WE CAN BEAT THEM!"* Cooper was laughing as the cacophony of utter, screaming madness whirled and raged about the cave. *"FOR EVER AND EVER!"* His eyes were locked onto the new celestial body. His voice was clear. *"OH WE CAN BE HER-"*

It was the last sound Coop or Ed ever heard.

The Mind's Tragedy

"Seven." Claire's voice was collected, calm. "You walk further into the field now, and the path begins to slowly narrow." She paused briefly. "It's late afternoon...the sun is starting to dip behind the horizon."

John lay on top of the made single bed, hands at his sides. His tan-colored leather jacket hung on the closed door's handle.

"Dusk descends, but you can still see everything in color. The forested fields are a rich, verdant green." Claire monitored his closed eyes and almost became hypnotized herself watching his sheathed pupils drifting side to side.

"Six. The foliage is sinking into a deeper and deeper green. You follow the path further on. Ahead you see dense woodland, full of greens and blues which are darker still." She had known John for five, maybe six years. Somewhere along the line he had graduated from 'boyfriend of a friend' to simply 'friend'. Claire kept her voice low and controlled. "You reach the edge of the woods, and begin to journey inside. It is lush, calming and totally serene." She took a slow breath. "You feel deeply at peace with the woods around you."

Claire had approached John about the session the week before. Her psych class was writing regressive hypnosis scripts and she was looking for a test subject. "Five." John was only too keen to volunteer for the assignment. "You continue to walk through the forest as it grows deeper and darker." Claire asked him to think of an incident he couldn't quite recall, something to serve as the focus for the session. He had mentioned something about a helicopter. "The path remains clear, but the canopy grows thicker overhead. You are totally alone, proceeding further into the inviting shadows."

"I'm not alone."

Claire jumped in her seat a little. The subject was not supposed to be talking at this point. And he was definitely not supposed to be having free-roaming thoughts. "No John, there's only you in the forest. The green is rich and dense, and its making you feel very sleepy."

"No, there's something behind the tree. Under it, in the dark. It's pale, and it doesn't have a head...or it does and I can't...I can't see it."

Claire's eyes widened, but she took a deep breath and moved on when he stopped rambling. "Four." She closed her eyes and steadied her breathing. "You keep walking through the woodland. Look at your feet John, you're slowly walking along the path." She opened her eyes again and looked at her friend: he was calming too, falling back under the suggestive spell of her words. "You look up from your feet now, further along the path; you see a very old stone well set in the ground." He breathed steadily again. "The path leads to the well and you lean on it, feeling the deep, cool stone. You sit on the edge of the well and look down into a beautiful, embracing darkness." John made a murmuring sound, like he had just sipped a hot drink on a cold morning.

"Three." Claire moistened her lips in the silence. "You slide gently into the well, almost as if in slow motion. The dark greens deepen slowly into black." She had asked John about any further details he recalled about the night of the helicopter incident, but he barely had any besides a few: an aircraft flying too close to suburban houses, a girlfriend who wouldn't wake up, and a strange experience in the garden which he recalled least of all. Claire had never heard about any of it before, which made it a good topic for the experiment. Less chance of guiding the subject. "You feel happy and safe and warm as you slide deeper into the dark."

"Two." Claire glanced around the room, her small house's second bedroom. It more or less served as a store-room, but tonight she had tidied it, modified the ambiance a little. Four tea-light candles sat on the bed head and provided light for the proceedings. The room still felt a little too dim though. "The darkness is yours John, it is sacred and thick. You slide deeper and deeper into the womb of the earth. You feel yourself cradled gently in the amniotic fluid." Claire made a quick mental note to edit that line out of her finished assignment. "As you approach the center of the black, you feel yourself slowing, *slowing*, *slowing*..." She slurred the word further each time, watching John's breathing and eye movements closely. He seemed in a state of absolute relaxation.

"One." She paused briefly. "You are now fully asleep, but able to talk to me and describe anything you see." Claire mentally crossed her fingers. "Can you hear me John?" Nothing. "John?"

"Yes. Yeah, I'm here." His voice sounded younger somehow, like he would have as a teenager. Not quite afraid, but unsure of himself. Fragile. Still, he seemed to be under. So far so good.

"John, I want you to go back to the night of the helicopter. Do you remember you were telling me about it the other day?" She felt awkward. She had never talked to a friend like this before, had never felt a person under her power so obviously. She wasn't so sure she liked it.

John's face remained motionless but he answered back almost immediately. "Yeah, I know the night." He nodded softly and Claire heard the pillow rustle in the silence. "I couldn't sleep which is how I saw it." His face looked like a waxen mask in the candlelight. The very corners of his lips turned up in a half-smile.

"OK, I want you to go back to just *before* you saw the helicopter, John. What are you doing?"

"There's...umm... there's like, a *lot* of dishes. The front of my shirt is wet from the suds." He frowned. "There's water all on me, I don't like it much." His frown spread into a gradual body squirm.

"It's alright John, it's alright." Claire inwardly marveled at her newly discovered 'therapist voice'. "Are you doing the washing up when you see the helicopter?"

"No, no...no, I *hear* it first. It keeps getting louder and I keep waiting for it to go over...c'mon, go over." His eyebrows furrowed. "Go over, go over...it just keeps getting *louder*." He sounded puzzled. "I pick up a tea-towel. Now I'm at the lounge room window. The tree is in the way outside." He frowned. "I can see lights."

"Is the sound coming from the lights?"

"Yeah, it's like...I dunno, maybe a helicopter? It's getting really loud now. I wonder if it will wake people up." John's eyes, beneath his lids, roamed slowly from side to side. "God, it's *huge*. Oh my god...how is it so *low*? How can they fly that here? It's just *hovering* there. And it's three in the morn- Lara? Hey, why won't she wake up? Lara!" Lara was John's girlfriend. He was getting upset. "*LARA!*"

"OK John, I want you to breathe slowly and deeply with me, like this." Claire breathed loudly, in and out, in and out. It took a handful of seconds but John started following along. The tension began to leave his body. "You're not there now, you're safe, very safe and warm and comfortable." Claire tried to make her voice sound as controlled as possible. "From this safe place you can look back there and tell me what happened, but you don't have to be scared by it." His face had turned motionlessness. To wax. "John, do you feel a little better now?"

"Yeah, I'm alright I guess. It's just...she won't wake up, even though the plane is so loud, and I'm yelling her name right near her head."

"John, I thought it was a helicopter?"

"Yeah, I dunno what it is, but flying around here at three in the morning and they'll get yelled at alright. Heck, someone might throw rocks at them or who knows what else."

Claire had never heard John, or any of her friends, for that matter, say 'heck' before. She worried he was confounding a childhood memory with the recent incident. Did kids even say heck?

"John, are you in the house on Ashleigh Street?"

"Yeah, that's where I am. 77 Ashleigh." He nodded again. "I've stopped trying to wake Lara up. I'm at the lounge room window."

"Can you see the plane?"

"It's going away now. I can't see anything through the trees." He frowned. "I can still hear it, but it's going... I'll go outside and see if anyone else woke up." John's body remained still but his eyes raced beneath his lids. "What? How is there nobody, there's *nobody*."

"Where are you standing?" Claire tried to take notes but they were scraps of phrases and words jotted here and there. She wasn't prepared for how much emotion could be involved in a hypnosis session. Maybe she wouldn't do friends from now on.

"I'm at the fence. The front gate...I almost tripped down the stairs, it's so damn dark."

"Is it a cloudy night, John? Is that why it's so dark?" Silence. Claire tried again. "Can you see the stars, or the moon?"

"Not from under the tree. Uh...now. Yeah, now I'm at the gate, and I can see a *lot* of stars. There's hardly any clouds. And no people. How could they not *wake up*? I'm alone out here." John's hand moved a little at his side, but returned to it's resting place. His expression grew less anxious. "I'm going back inside. I've still got the tea-towel in my hand. There are suds everywhere."

"You're back inside now?"

"Yeah, but I need to change my shirt cause it's too wet. I didn't know how wet it is, it's making me feel...but maybe I should finis-*shit! What was that?"* John's face went from calm to terrified in a transition that made Claire feel sick. *"Fuck, there's something here!"*

"It's alright, John, *it's alright.* You're in the woods, the sacred woods, in the center of a safe and encompassing womb. Nothing can hurt you from here, you're in total control. You're in control, John."

"I'm in control."

"You're in control." Claire breathed deeply herself and wondered if she should just try to end the session. It seemed he was confusing memories, possibly overlapping them with an unexplained or half-forgotten incident that had long ago inspired a similar terror. She knew John would want to know more though, especially about what happened in the garden. He'd ask her why she ended the session, why she bailed out, and then she'd feel guilty. So Claire took another deep breath instead. *Therapist mode.* "Now, from this safe vantage point, I want you to describe to me what made you feel like you weren't alone." She quickly added, "Remember – these things can't hurt you."

John started nodding again; the pillow resumed its rustling song. "Footsteps." He was resolute. And then not. "Or...a shuffling sound? Out in the yard. I flick the kitchen curtain open, the one above the sink. Yeah. I can see it in the moonlight. But..." He paused for a long time. "It's just gone so fast."

"What do you see?" Claire leaned forward in her seat. "Play it back slowly so that you can describe it to me in detail."

His brow furrowed. "Nah, it looks..." He seemed confused, disgusted even. "It looks wrong. It's all...bent over. I don't think I remember seeing this part before." He seemed to be at least somewhat distancing himself from the event. More in control of his emotions than a few minutes ago.

"Is it a person?"

"No, it's too big...or...it moves wrong." His face was absolutely still. "It's like an eel."

"It looks like an eel?"

"No, it just moves like one. But more *crinkled.* Like legs, or feelers."

"Does it ha-"

"No." John's head shook. "*NO!* I don't want to look at it anymore, I'm not supposed to look at this bit. I'll talk about the next bit, but I'm not going to look out the kitchen window anymore." His voice was atonal, but firm.

"OK John, we don't have to look out the kitchen window any longer." Claire quickly scribbled down a sentence on her notepad. "What did you do after that?"

"I got the bokken."

"What?" Claire looked up from the notes she was furiously trying to write. Her voice had slipped from therapist to friend. She gathered herself. "What did you get, John?"

"Sword. It's a wooden sword...for practice. Lara's still asleep."

"Are you trying to wake her?"

"Nah, I'm just getting the bokken. My shirt's still really wet. It's making me...I feel wet and scared. I'm about to head out the front door."

"I want you to slow down with me a second John. This next part is really important, you want to remember what you saw, so I need you to take some deep breaths with me." He mirrored each of the seven slow breaths she took. "OK, now describe to me what you see."

"It's dark...I'm on the porch. Yeah, but I'm under the pine tree, so the moonlight can't get to me. Wait...is there a moon? Maybe it's starlight."

"And what can you see from the porch, John?"

"I can see out into the yard. Hmm, nothing wrong...wait... I need to take the washing in."

Claire smiled to herself. "Do you still have the sword with you? The bokken?"

"Yeah." His voice quickened. "I'm rubbing my palms on the dry part of my shirt. They're real sweaty. OK, I'm good now." He slowed down again. "It's really dark here. I don't want to trip down the stairs." Worry began to gather on John's face.

"It's alright, you can't be hurt, remember?" He was silent. She paused a moment, unsure of how to spur him on without *leading* him on, which was the well-known pitfall of the regressive technique. "Do you have a light with you?" She instantly regretted the poor choice of question, but John didn't take the bait.

"Nah, the flashlight's inside. Phone too." His right hand twitched. "I'm down the steps now. The path's tricky. I'm using the bokken to feel the way. Wow, it's so bright. I can almost make out colors." Awe dripped from his voice, which was now almost dry of fear. "There's not even a moon, it's just the stars."

"Slow down for me John; what are you doing now?"

"Well, I can see OK, except where there's shade under the trees." More hand twitching. "I'm walking over to the neighbor's fence now."

"Number 79 or 75?"

"Umm...75. No, wait, 79. You know, the one with the old guy...he draws with highlighters on his dog." It seemed bokkens weren't the only thing Claire had yet to learn about. "I'm leaning over the old guy's fence now. I think I'm looking for a certain star...*hey!*" John's voice had lowered to a fierce whisper. "... *can you see that thing?*"

"What are you looking at John?" Claire readied her pen. "Describe it for me."

"It's the stars, but they're moving." His face scrunched up in confusion. His fists very slowly clenched and unclenched on the bed. "No, no there's something moving in front of the stars...some *shape*." John lifted his head off the pillow, as if straining to see through the flesh of his eyelids. "*No... NO!*" Suddenly his head dropped back on the pillow. A strange grimace conquered his face and Claire could make out tears forming at the corners of his eyes. "*It's asking me to come over to it!*" He sobbed gently while still seeming in control of his emotions. "I'm walking over to it, but I'm shaking...I'm shaking so much." He continued crying quietly. The attitude of his voice made it sound to Claire like he was recounting a particularly emotional movie.

"Where are you walking now, John?"

"I'm stepping through the garden. I'm walking over to the corner, to the trees in the corner of the yard." The tears subsided and again he seemed to be trying to look through closed eyes. "It's dark here. The dirt in the garden is soft under my feet, really soft. *Oh fuck!*" For a moment John's eyes flashed open to stare blankly at the ceiling. Claire quickly hopped off her chair and leaned over him, placing a hand on his shoulder.

"Sh, it's OK John, just close your eyes. There, that's it. Lay back and breathe deeply." She gave him an example to follow. She watched the rising and falling of his chest, watched it slow, before removing her hand and sitting back on the chair. She put the notebook down beside her. This was getting too much. "We're going to come back out now John, I want y-"

"It has these folds on it...like a mushroom..." His voice was barely a whisper, but it was enough to stop Claire short. The tears had stopped, his face frozen in a bizarre mixture of terror and awe. "I don't... I can't understand."

"Describe to me where you're standing, John, what you're seeing." Curiosity replaced her worry almost instantaneously. She picked her notepad up. "Are you under the trees, too?"

"No." His voice had risen to a quiet speaking level. "No, I'm in the starlight. I'm standing in starlight. And, I didn't mean to. I've broken some of the tomato plants." He frowned. "Did we bury the dog down here?"

"John, you're seeing the night when you stood in the backyard and something was under the trees, hidden in the shadows. The night of the helicopter. Can you tell m-"

"*We have come from between.*"

Claire's jaw dropped faster than her pen. Her friend's voice had radically changed in timbre, tone, and personality. She'd heard of subordinate personality traits emerging in hypnotic sessions, often personified into loose 'characters', but this had markings of a completely dissociated personality. She picked her pen back up and took a new page. Her voice was a little shaky. "Am I still speaking with John?"

"*Two...three...five...*" His voice had a strange polyphonic quality, like it was under-laid with a rattling, buzzing drone. Shivers raced up and down Claire's spine. "*Eighty-nine...two hundred and thirty-three...*" John's breathing remained perfectly calm, his eyes closed, his hands relaxed. The droning part of his voice sounded like it was coming from his chest, the rattle of some otherworldly infection. "*Twenty-eight thousand, six hundred and fifty-seven...*"

Claire didn't know what to say, write, or do. She started to jot down the number that had just left John's lips, only to have him fall silent once again. His eyes traced with infinite slowness from beneath his lids, one side to the other. The tea-light candles flickered. Slowly, John's pupils began making the return journey, silent sentinels on a skin desert. Without warning, the dual voices resumed speaking. *"There is One who resides at the bottom of a deep river, in the West. Many tall pines grow nearby."*

A wave of nausea rolled over Claire. Her limbs felt shaky and useless. Her friend's new voice had a hideous kind of *calmness* to it; a naturalness amongst the unnaturalness of it. She fought the urge to violently and spontaneously vomit. "I don't..."

"They are known as Acrile."

Tears formed in Claire's eyes. "I don't know what you...John..." A distinct quality in the buzz that came from his throat, from his chest, drove her senses into total revolt. She stood up and clapped twice, loudly, the signal to John's unconscious mind that let him know to come back. To wake up. But there was no response. She clapped again, louder this time. John's eyes opened.

The sickening, rattling chest-drone reached a higher pitch. *"Algol ascends above the horizon."* John sat up, swiveled his legs over the side of the bed, and stood. Claire watched, frozen, as her friend walked over to the room's south wall and stood, staring at it. His nose was an inch or two away from the wall. Silence. He stood like that for maybe twenty seconds, seemingly staring through the wall and miles beyond. Light-years beyond. Claire's mind flashed back to when his eyes were closed, when it was his pupils peering through skin. Now, his eyes seemed to look through the wall itself. And then, as if the preceding half-hour didn't exist, John looked to his left, to his friend. "Why am I standing here?"

Claire started laughing, but not happy laughing. She felt a prickle of insanity flood through her after what just happened. Then it all hit her, what she'd heard and how it scared the wits out of her.

She looked at John and collapsed into wracking tears.

****

Session notes:

Script followed, minimal improv. John went straight under; possibly highly suggestible.

Abnormal behavior during countdown (after 5, before 4). Projection. Unexplored trauma?

Spatial confusion. Inconsistent recall re:

Claire stopped typing and whipped her head around to see where the sound came from. There was nothing. She turned around in her seat and held her breath, straining to catch any clue of the sound's origin. Still nothing. Probably just rats in the attic again. She got up from the computer desk and walked over to the kitchen sink, glancing at the microwave clock's digital readout. Bed or coffee? She turned the tap on and started filling the jug.

John left a good two hours ago. He had stayed awhile, listening in disbelief to how he acted and what he said while under hypnosis. Neither of them had really believed it would be so easy, although both agreed that further sessions were out of the question. At least for the time being. She didn't even want to finish typing up the last few hundred words of session notes; all she kept hearing was the tone of that god-awful *buzz* that spoke in tandem with John's voice. She felt sick all over again.

THUMP. Claire let out a scream. Something crashed loudly into the second bedroom window. Somehow, it wasn't followed by the blistering crack of shattered glass. There was silence. Claire closed her eyes and took two deep breaths, in through the nose, out through the mouth. In through the nose, out through the mouth. She put down the now-full jug, grabbed the magnetized flashlight off the fridge, and turned to face the front door. The window of the second bedroom would be immediately on her right if she walked outside; whatever had crashed into it was probably still lying there. Claire took another breath and tried not to let the thought rise.

Or standing there.

She crossed the kitchen and then the sun-room, reaching the front door in five long strides. *I can't hesitate, or I'm going to give myself a panic attack.* She distantly noted how bad her hand trembled as it neared the door's lock. *I wish I had a bokken instead of a fucking flashlight.* Anxiety condensed into a tight ball in the pit of Claire's stomach, giving her the final push she needed into action: she blustered through the door, hoisting the light around in an exaggerated arc like she was drunkenly drawing a pistol, and fired the flash's beam at the window. There was nothing there, just a scuff mark. *Wait...*

At the upper edge of the smudge was a feather, smeared with blood. She aimed the narrow cone of light at the ground and saw its once-owner – a small huddled mass on the dirt. Claire didn't bother to walk over and find out what kind of bird it was. She looked up at the night sky and her thoughts quickly gravitated toward internet reading she'd been doing not an hour beforehand.

Algol. Science may have called it an 'eclipsing binary star', but to the ancient and desert-haunted Arabic peoples it was the head of the ghoul. *The Demon-star.* Why had John named it during the session? Part of the constellation Perseus, Algol was due to rise around one a.m., which was less than three hours away. Yet, it was a later realization that had made Claire feel the beginnings of true dread. When John, entranced, stood up from the bed and looked 'through' the wall he would have been looking just about at the point where Algol was to rise above the horizon. *Demon-star.* She hurried back inside and slammed the door loudly behind her, sealing herself inside the relative safety of her house. *Or is it safe?* She locked the door and – unusually, for her – secured the deadbolt as well. She leaned her back against the wood, trying to reassure herself of its thickness, and considered her next move. *Screw the coffee.* She went to bed.

****

Claire woke slowly. Very slowly (*One*). It felt like she had been trapped under dark, swirling waters, and she was only now (*Two*) able to break through the ocean's surface of slumber and into the waking air. She let her eyes adjust (*Three*), thankful that she had left the window and curtains ajar. The night breeze was refreshing as it slid into her lungs (*Four*). The bedroom ceiling came steadily into focus, a beam of moonlight (*Five*) slicing through the shadows. It reminded her of the flash-light's beam (*Six*). She let this thought linger on for a moment (*Seven*). Claire was awake.

She leaned over to look at what time it was. Only, she didn't. She couldn't move.

Sleep paralysis.

Claire remained relatively calm, despite the circumstances. It didn't qualify as 'recurrent isolated sleep paralysis', but she had experienced this feeling at least a half-dozen times before. Besides which, it was par for the psychology course to at least be acquainted with the phenomena.

It's OK, I must have been dreaming, then I woke suddenly. Claire studied the beam of moonlight that streaked her ceiling. *My muscles think I'm still dreaming, so they'll take a while to wake up.*

She began to explore the peripheries of her vision, distantly noting the dim shapes around her room as they gently outlined themselves.

It's taken twenty minutes to regain control before, so there's no need to panic. Just let it flow.

The chest of drawers revealed its hulking profile. The single couch began to follow suit, a living Rorschach test passing away into gradual visual realization. But the inkblot that was supposed to be her couch looked different somehow. More angled. *Am I hallucinating?*

From somewhere behind her and to the left, Claire heard a low drone. *Oh my god.* She struggled to control her breathing. The drone became louder, throatier. *Fuck. FUCK.* Her heart slammed into her chest and throat with such force that she thought she must be visibly shaking. The drone grew louder, closer. More familiar. If Claire could have moved at that moment, she would have laughed. She did the next best thing and rolled her eyes in the dark. *It's a fucking plane!* She caught sight of the aircraft's pulsing red tail-light as it courted the night sky; it was gone again in an instant due to the angle she was afforded. She breathed a sigh of relief. It shook with happiness, not fear.

Claire's mental grin grew into a grimace. The couch. Her eyes darted back to the foot of the bed. *C'mon, c'mon.* She held her breath and waited for her vision to recover from the light exposure. It didn't take long. The strange angle was definitely still there.

Fuck, what's going on?

Claire knew if she panicked overmuch, there was a chance she would prolong the paralysis. She tried to make out details of the angle, to locate the error in the couch's logic. Without warning, there was partial clarity. Claire's sudden intake of breath broke the newly formed silence. It was a humanoid figure on the couch. It looked pale.

Hallucinations are a common part of the sleep paralysis experience. Claire closed her eyes and tried to reign in her ragged gasps for air. *You've had them before, you're having them again. You've had them before, you're having them again.*

Her mind and heart pounded ceaselessly. Her eyes snapped open, watering in unadulterated animal terror. The figure stood. It moved closer, and the moonlight revealed a lurid, mustard glow. It seemed she knew its tone, like it had haunted her, that color. And finally: clarity. It was John's leather jacket. Claire tried to speak his name, to scream it, but she couldn't even raise a murmur. Now that he walked into the moonlight's steady glow, she saw her friend's face appeared utterly lifeless. Waxen.

"Algol ascends above the horizon."

Despite the paralysis, her internal organs revolted. Her mind most of all. She couldn't hear John's voice. Only the buzzing. The unnatural suggestion of human speech, droning through the bedroom air. Articulate electricity. Claire felt her legs swing themselves over the side of the bed, cross the room, and stand an inch away from the room's south wall. She still had no control of her body. She knew what she'd be looking at if she could see through the wall. Her mind struggled in vain to hold onto a single thought for more than a fraction of a second. From the periphery of her vision, she became aware of John shuffling to her side through the shadows. He stood slightly behind her, his face inches from her left shoulder. His pale skin appeared folded or wrinkled in some way, like a mushroom.

"Acrile."

The buzz eclipsed everything in her head. It held her mind down, forcing its sickly sound through her soul.

"*Acrile, Acrile, Acrile.*"

As the drone engulfed her, her mind, the bedroom wall began to flicker and fade. She could see through it and realized now what she saw was not moonlight, but starlight, bright and piercing. She could see the starlight. The demon-star glowing through the measureless reaches of space, through the endless rolling infinities.

"*Acrile, Acrile, Acrile.*"

The rattling buzz took her to it, to its head, to the ravenous cosmic ghoul.

"*ACRILE, ACRILE, ACRILE.*"

The drone-voice became the vessel for her mind. In seconds she strode the far-flung aethyr, moved through the watery wombs of space. Now, she was one of many, her soul dragged in against its will to become another slave for the demon star. Soon it would have enough power to do what must be done, and Claire was helpless against its strength. She was nothing more than a thought in the mind of Algol. As fear consumed her, the one known as Claire was no more.

"*ACRILE.*"

Made in the USA
Monee, IL
09 July 2021